VENGEANCE

CARFANO CRIME FAMILY
BOOK 3

REBECCA GANNON

newsletter, blog, shop, and links to all social media:
www.rebeccagannon.com

Content Warning
This book is intended for those 18 and over, containing graphic violence that may make some readers uncomfortable and has references to past sexual assault that may pose as a trigger to some readers.

More by Rebecca Gannon

Pine Cove
Her Maine Attraction
Her Maine Reaction
Her Maine Risk
Her Maine Distraction

Carfano Crime Family
Casino King
The Boss
Vengeance
Executioner
Wild Ace

Standalone Novels
Whiskey & Wine
Redeeming His Reputation

To those who think they have no hope of escaping whatever it is keeping you from living, know that the universe will always bring you the key, even if it's in a way or within a person you never expected.

This is for you.

THE CARFANO FAMILY

Leo (d)
(m) Katarina (d)

Michael (d)	Salvatore (d)	Anthony	Richard	Maria
(m) Anita	(m) Teresa	(m) Francesca	(m) Christina	(m) Carmine
Leo, Alec, Luca, Katarina	Nico, Vincenzo, Mia	Stefano, Marco, Gabriel	Saverio, Gia, Aria	Matteo, Elena

(m) – married / (d) – deceased

"It's a fear of telling people everything inside you
because you are afraid it's too ugly for them to hear
You are afraid it will ruin them to know
But each day you stay silent
it's ruining you"

- Courtney Peppernell
"Pillow Thoughts III"

CHAPTER 1
Angela

Sorting through my nail polish box, I pick out my favorite – Hot Tamale – and settle in on the center of my bed. I've gotten pretty good at painting my nails since going to a salon hasn't been an option for quite some time.

My father has kept me and the rest of the family under lock and key for the past five years while he's descended into a state of what I can only describe as manic paranoia. He thinks everyone is out to get him, and doesn't trust anyone that isn't blood related.

But even I know that those who are can't always be trusted either.

And while I hate being trapped inside this house like a

prisoner, never being allowed to go anywhere or do anything outside of the thick stone walls of the compound, I'm also grateful. Grateful for the ability to finally be able to sleep through the night without the shaking fear of the door creaking open at some point, and grateful that the nightmares that used to plague me nightly have become few and far between.

Only when there's a severe thunderstorm do they return, and I wake up gasping for air in a cold sweat, searching the shadows of my room in the flashes of lightning.

It's been a few weeks since my last one, and today has been a relatively good day for me, so I'm finishing it off with a pedicure. I roamed the garden this morning and then found a quiet corner to read before we had an early Sunday dinner on the patio under the pergola. The Autumn sun shone gold and orange before dipping behind the tree line.

It's at that point where the days are still hanging onto the last of the summer's warmth and the nights dip in temperature, bringing with it the cool crisp bite of the impending winter months. Then it'll be back to being stuck inside this mansion trying not to go crazy with nowhere to go, passing my time with the few hobbies I'm allowed to have.

I don't know how much longer I can do this.

I'm trapped in a gilded cage locked from the outside, with the key held firmly in my father's grasp.

He'll never let me go.

He'll never let me see the outside of these walls so long as he's alive.

I don't know what made him relocate us full-time to our Long Island home from the city and lock us inside, but it's been five years, and I've learned to stop asking. Asking only resulted in me having the chance to refine my makeup skills at covering up bruises.

Staying quiet and out of sight is the best way to skirt the wrath of my father. But even when I'm out of sight, I'm still watched. There are cameras everywhere, as well as a full-time security team that roams the grounds and live in the house on the back end of the property. The only place there aren't cameras or security is the hallway of mine and my father's bedrooms. He wants to keep a close eye on everyone else, but doesn't want anyone to be able to do the same to him. Especially in his private quarters.

As the only daughter to the head of the Cicariello crime family, I was raised under a constant watchful eye and taught to be what was expected of me – a pretty pawn in a game I wasn't allowed to know anything about.

When I was young and naïve, I assumed everyone's careful treatment of me was because they saw me as someone special and someone they loved dearly. But I was wrong. Everyone was in on the game but me. My mother tried helping me before she died, but I saw what my father did to her afterwards. And my two older brothers wouldn't dare go against what our father decreed, even if it meant knowing their little sister was being used as a stepping stone in their quest for more power and money.

Sucking in a deep breath, my hand shakes as I apply the first coat of red polish to my toe nails. Luckily, by the time

I've finished, I've breathed through the memories trying to creep into the forefront of my brain, and pushed them back down where they belong while the music I put on carries me to someplace far away.

Grabbing my Kindle, I sit on the seat below the window that looks out to the backyard and beyond. From the third floor, I can see to the edge of the property and the security team's house with all their lights on.

Books have been my escape for as long as I can remember. They're what saved me when I thought I had nothing and no one left. I could have the family I always wanted, I could have the adventures I've always dreamt of going on, and I could fall in love over and over again in ways I can only hope to one day myself.

But that love isn't real.

It's called fiction for a reason, and I use it for the break from reality that I need it to be, because I know I'll never escape the hell I'm in now.

No one would even hear me scream if I decided to.

It wouldn't help.

Nothing does.

I've accepted that this is the life I've been born into and have come to terms with the fact that I'll always be under my father's thumb. And after him, my brothers. I'm nothing to them but a bargaining chip to use, and a prize to give to those who side with them.

Leaning my head against the window, I close my eyes and let the cool glass relieve my suddenly heated skin, humming the tune of my favorite song. It's the one my mother used to sing to me to get me to go to sleep when I was little. She was the only one who tried to shelter me from the inevitable fate my life was heading towards.

A lone tear rolls down my cheek and I breathe in a shaky breath, trying to hold it together and calm my racing pulse. I promised myself a long time ago I wouldn't break down again. Tears don't get you anything but a deeper hole dug of your own making.

It was only when I felt the dirt start to fall on my head that I realized I was burying myself alive and I had to claw my way out before I suffocated.

I refuse to let what happened be the reason I die, and whatever fight I have left in me, I'm going to use it to cling onto the hope that I'll find a way to be free.

Blinking my eyes open, I take a deep breath and open to the book I was reading this afternoon.

I get lost in the dizzying plot twists that keep me on the edge of my seat, and just when I get to the part where the Hero is about to tell the Heroine how he truly feels after rescuing her from the hit squad that kidnapped her, the knob of my bedroom door begins to jiggle fiercely.

Panic sets in and I jump, my Kindle slipping from my hands and falling to the carpeted floor in a dull thud.

No.

No, this can't be happening.

Not after all this time.

My lungs constrict and my throat closes around my rapid, shallow breaths. Pulling my knees up to my chest, I wrap my arms around my legs and keep my eyes glued to the door.

The handle continues to move vigorously, and despite my legs shaking and having nothing to defend myself with, I stand up to face whoever is on the other side.

I swallow a scream that bubbles up when the door splinters open, and I press myself against the wall. Standing there is an imposing figure, tall and dark in the shadows, and when he steps through the doorway, I suck in a sharp breath.

I've never seen him before.

I would've remembered him.

His dark and piercing eyes meet mine before traveling the length of my body and back, going even darker.

I wish I was wearing flannel instead of a pair of sleep shorts and a tank top, leaving little to the imagination.

He takes a step towards me and I remain pressed against the wall, my eyes locked on his.

Swallowing hard, I manage to find my voice. "Who are you?"

He tilts his head slightly, studying me as if I'm a mystery he's trying to solve.

"Who are you?" I ask again, my voice stronger.

"Who are *you*?" he counters, taking another step closer.

"An-Angela." Damn it, I hate that my voice just waivered and I stuttered. I always did that as a kid when my father or brothers yelled at me.

"Angela Cicariello," he says more to himself than me. His eyes roam over my face and body again, and I fidget under his gaze, making him smirk. He takes note of every move I make.

When he takes another step towards me, I hold my hand up. "Don't come any closer. I don't care what kind of deal you made with my father, but you can't have me."

His brows clash together and his eyes meet mine again, this time filled with a thunderous anger. "What the fuck do you mean I can't have you?"

"You. Can't. Have. Me." For some reason, instead of cowering, I find myself feeling stronger, braver.

"Why do you think I want you?" he rumbles darkly, as if he's toying with me. "I came for your father, but I find you locked away here, too. Two for one."

"No." I shake my head. I've wanted to escape for years, but not to just be taken by someone else who'll bring me God knows where and do God knows what with me. At least here, I can lock myself away from all of that, even if I am still just a prisoner in my own home.

"You don't have a choice, *uccellino*." I blink up at him. I'm not familiar with that word, but I love the way it sounds rolling from his tongue in perfect Italian.

He may not know this, but I've never had a choice.

CHAPTER 2
Luca

Tonight's the night.

After years of waiting and plotting our revenge, we're finally going after that motherfucker Joey Cicariello. He's been hiding out in his Long Island home like a fucking pussy for the past five years, knowing that my family would one day come for him.

Joey had my father and uncle Sal killed, thinking he could take over our family's hold on the city's construction union and underground gambling rooms when we were at our most vulnerable without leadership. But to Joey's surprise, our father already had a plan in place for his demise.

My brother Leo was ready to take over for him, and he didn't miss a step. None of us did. We all knew our roles and were ready to step into them without hesitation.

Our Carfano name holds enough weight to crumble even the strongest of men when tested. But our father broke us long before we ever had the chance to be tested. He broke us himself in order to mold us into who he deemed fit to rule over the empire he built after our grandfather passed the reins to him. Each generation is meant to build upon the past's legacy, and my brothers, cousins, and myself have done just that.

Tonight is the culmination of the patience Leo instilled in us. We killed the men who were hired to kill our father and uncle, burned down the restaurants and gyms they owned, dismantled their prostitution business, and took over their hold on the trucking union. We took everything, which forced them to make drug deals like a common street gang to stay in the game.

Dom and Geno, Joey's sons, struck a deal last week to serve us their father on a silver platter in exchange for the shipment of weapons we intercepted. They've been using Leo's woman's charity to smuggle in drugs and weapons from Colombia as a go-between for the Latin Kings, and the only way to ensure her safety, while also not putting her name on the Latin Kings' hit list, was to make a deal with Dom and Geno. They want the freedom to come out of hiding with the promise we won't keep coming for them, and Leo wants Abrianna safe. It's give and take in our world. We just always make sure the outcome is in our favor. And this is no different.

I'm in an SUV with my brothers, Leo and Alec, on our way to the Cicariello compound while my cousins, Nico and Vinny, are in the one behind us, with two more in front with five men in each. Vinny and Nico are as invested in this mission as Leo, Alec and I since their father was the one Joey took out alongside ours.

Even though our fathers were bastards and raised us to be the monsters we are today, no one fucks with our family and gets away with it. That would show weakness. And Carfanos are anything but weak.

Stefano is one of our captains, but he's also our resident hacker, and he's in a car right outside of the compound to disable the Cicariello's security system and anything else that might stand in our way. Gabriel and Marco, our other captains, are with the truck of confiscated guns in a nearby abandoned lot with another five of our soldiers, ready for the exchange when they get the word.

As Leo's underboss, it's my job to protect him at all costs. But I'm also his brother, and I'll do whatever I have to to keep him even remotely sane. And Abrianna is that for him. She's the one thing in this world that has the power to bring my brother to his knees. She gave him back his humanity. The same goes for Tessa with Alec.

It's silent in the car and silent over the air of our linked intercoms.

As we get closer, the walls surrounding the Cicariello compound come into view and I feel my blood rush a little faster through my veins. I'm ready for this. I've always loved this part of the life — the action. I can be the calmest motherfucker around ninety percent of the time, but that's only because I get my recklessness out in spades the other ten percent.

"Approaching now. You ready, Stef?" Leo says over the coms.

"Yeah," he replies. "Security cameras have been cut and anyone checking will see a continuous loop of nothing."

"Good."

"I've overridden their control of the gate, and it should be opening in 3, 2, 1…"

"Car 1, go," Leo says, and our caravan of SUVs flood through the gate and down the long gravel drive towards the gaudy monstrosity of a house that son-of-a-bitch has been locked away in. "Let's fucking do this. You know your jobs, everyone."

Pulling the magazine from my gun to triple check it's loaded, I roll my neck from side to side and see my brothers doing the same.

Cut from the same cloth.

When our SUV comes to a stop outside of the front door, Leo, Alec and I wait for our soldiers to first take their places before Vinny, Nico, and the rest of us join them.

Dante, our family's hitter, takes the tactical lead and signals two of our soldiers inside before him, with the rest of us following suit.

Dom and Geno made sure the doors were left open for us, and we slip inside undetected.

We were told that every Sunday, the immediate family

has dinner together while the guards have their own in a house on the back part of the compound. And after every Sunday dinner, Joey has a massage in his room, which is in a private section of the house. He won't be guarded, and it's the one part of the house not under surveillance because he's so paranoid. He doesn't want anyone, even his own men, to spy on him.

Fucking idiot. It just makes it easier for us to go in undetected.

Walking up the marble staircase to the second floor, we move in tight formation through the halls along the route we mapped out from the blueprints we were given.

We pass room after room, all unoccupied, and by the looks of it, haven't been for quite some time.

"Approaching the bedroom now," Leo says over the coms.

"No movement in the rest of the house," Stefano replies, monitoring their security feed.

Dante, in the lead, kicks the door in, and four soldiers follow him inside. I hear a woman shriek and Joey yell, "Who the fuck are you? How did you get in here?"

I watch Leo's face turn to stone and his eyes flare with fire before walking into the room and facing the man he's picked apart and driven into hiding.

"Good to see you again, Joey. It's been a while."

"How the fuck did you get in here, Leo?" he growls, his eyes darting around to each of us before him.

"That's not for you to worry about. Get dressed. You're coming with me."

"Like hell I am," Joey scoffs, sitting up from the massage table.

"You have one minute to put some fucking clothes on."

And he better do it quickly. I don't want to see any more of his paunchy old ass for longer than I have to. I know he's been held up in here for five years, but it looks like he hasn't seen the sun or taken care of himself in the same amount of time.

"You know," Joey starts, putting his clothes on, "I thought you'd have come for me a long time ago."

"I needed time to dismantle everything you built," Leo says, crossing his arms. "I'm a patient man. My father taught me that."

Joey laughs manically. "I'm sure he did."

That fucking bastard. He's going to find out soon how much our father taught us. From the age of ten, we were raised to be Carfano men – strong, resilient, resourceful, cunning, and most importantly, deadly. All of those elements make us who we are and are woven into our DNA, shaping us into the men we need to be to remain at the top.

"You need to hurry. There's movement on the south east side of the property," Stefano informs us.

"Clear a path back for us," Leo orders. "Let's fucking go," he says to the rest of us in the room.

Dante grabs Joey, binding his hands behind his back with zip ties before shoving him forward. Filing out of the room, everyone goes to the right, but as the last one, I sweep my eyes down the other end of the hall, and something seems off.

Peeling away from the pack, I walk in the opposite direction, something pulling me towards a room where light seeps out from the crack under the door. This is supposed to be Joey's private section of the house. Who does he have here with him?

The only other light comes from Joey's room behind me, cloaking me in the shadows, and as I approach the room, I wonder what the fuck I'm doing. Everyone else has already headed back the way we came and I don't have backup, but I don't give a fuck.

I test the knob. It's locked.

I don't hear any movement on the other side, but I need to know what secret Joey is keeping behind this door.

I keep trying the handle, hoping it'll give way under my force, but it doesn't. Frustrated and short on time, I step back and kick the door in.

My eyes immediately zero in on a figure pressed against the far wall, and I take her in. All of her. She's wearing a pair of pink shorts that give me a view of the entirety of her long legs, and a white tank top that's so thin, I can see her nipples poking through the fabric.

Her face is free of makeup and her hair is piled on top of her head in a knot, giving me an unobstructed view of her delicate features. She's young, maybe eighteen or nineteen, which means she's probably too young for me to be having the reaction I am to her.

My blood rushes through me, making my cock swell in an instant.

She's fucking beautiful.

Exquisite.

Angelic.

And despite how small she appears, she doesn't cower under my stare. She stands her ground, looking back at me with shielded eyes.

Taking a step closer, I keep my eyes on hers, hoping to see more than she's giving me, which is nothing at the moment.

I watch her slim throat work as she swallows before her lips move, asking, "Who are you?"

Tilting my head to the side, I study her, her soft voice filled with wavering confidence. "Who are you?" she repeats.

"Who are *you?*" I counter, needing to know her name.

"An-Angela," she stammers, then pinches her lips together.

"Angela Cicariello," I muse, raking my eyes down her body again, taking in every inch of skin on display.

Well, fuck me. The little Cicariello girl sure has grown up. I saw her in pictures years ago. They were surveillance photos my father had on Joey, and I remember because it was rare to see him and her together. My father hadn't even realized he had a daughter before that, and she was around eleven or twelve in the photos.

Stepping closer to her, I see a flash of fear in her eyes, and I take great satisfaction in that. I want her afraid. I want her to show me any emotion other than the false confidence she's trying to embody. Anyone else would've screamed or called for help by now, but she hasn't. It's almost as if she knows no one would come for her even if she did. And for

15

some reason, that makes me fucking furious.

What did she have to endure to know she was on her own, even with a man like me kicking her door down?

She holds her hand up. "Don't come any closer. I don't care what kind of deal you made with my father, but you can't have me."

Confused, my voice comes out angrier than I mean it to when I ask, "What the fuck do you mean I can't have you?"

"You. Can't. Have. Me," she grits out.

"Why do you think I want you? I came for your father, but I find you locked away here too. Two for one."

"No." She shakes her head, her eyes turning glassy.

"You don't have a choice, *uccellino*," I rumble, not knowing where the fuck that came from. She just reminds me of a scared little bird, caged in this room. "Let's go." Taking the last few strides to close the distance between us, I grab her arm and pull her towards the door, ignoring the fire I feel from touching her soft skin.

She flinches at my touch, but I don't let go.

Dragging her out of the room, I lead her down the hall, and she fights me the entire way. We make it to the first set of stairs when I hear Stefano yell through our coms that a guard is rounding the corner on them downstairs, right before I hear the first of the shots ring out.

Angela gasps and fights me more. I get distracted trying to listen in to what's going on that she catches me off guard and gets the drop on me. Stomping on my foot, she squats down and elbows me in the fucking dick, and I lose my grip on her. With the wind knocked out of me, I brace myself on

16

the wall as she takes off down the hall.

Fuck!

Running after her, I smile maniacally to myself. I love a good chase.

She looks back at me with wide eyes and darts into the first room she comes upon, slamming and locking it just as I reach her.

Growling, I step back and kick the door in. Angela lets out a soft cry and covers her mouth with her hand.

"Did you think I wouldn't do that twice?" I taunt as she scrambles backwards. I prowl forward and flash her a triumphant grin when the backs of her knees hit the edge of a bed.

"Please don't," she begs, her voice breaking. "Please don't do this. Whatever my father promised you, I won't do it."

I stop short. Why the fuck is she saying this again? "And what exactly do you think he promised me?"

Confusion flashes in her eyes, but she quickly covers it up. This girl doesn't let me see much. I open my mouth to ask her again, but I hear Leo yell over the coms to find me.

"Let's go." Grabbing her arm again, I pull her from the bed. "Your father promised me nothing. And there's nothing he could ever promise me that would change what's coming for him."

"What are you talking about? Who are you?"

Walking her down the hall again, we're about to round the last corner that will bring us back to the main staircase in the foyer when I turn on her and press her against the wall.

Her soft curves melt against me and I stifle a groan as I rasp in her ear, "The son of the man your father had killed."

The sound of her sucking in a sharp breath has me picturing her making that same sound when she sees my cock for the first time and wonders how it'll fit in her tiny body.

Fuck.

Hating myself for even thinking that, I push away from her.

She's off limits.

She's Joey's fucking daughter for Christ's sake. She's leverage and that's it. I'm taking her for leverage. I repeat that in my head as I take her down the stairs, trying to convince myself that I'm not taking her for any other reason as we avoid the dead bodies and pools of blood on our way out to the waiting SUV.

Opening the trunk, I lift her up and inside. The feel of her warm body in my hands makes me want to lift her and sit her on my lap instead, but I slam the door closed. On her, and those thoughts.

Climbing in next to Leo, I feel his pissed-off eyes burning a hole in the side of my head.

"Alfie, go," Leo barks angrily, and his driver/bodyguard takes off up the driveway.

"All men are out and accounted for," Stefano says over the coms when we clear the front gate.

Leo rips his out of his ear and pulls his phone from his pocket. "Make the exchange," he says to Marco or Gabriel, and then hangs up.

Angela sniffs behind us and Leo turns to me. "There

better be a good fucking reason for this."

"Later," is all I say, and he doesn't push me further. I don't want to deal with his shit right now, especially when I don't have answers to the questions I know he's going to ask.

I just took Angela fucking Cicariello from her home.

On impulse.

Without an order to do so.

I'm not entirely sure if I rescued or kidnapped her. But either way, she's mine now.

The sound of her teeth clattering has me turning to check on her, and something in me twists when I see her shaking. She's either in shock or cold from wearing next to nothing.

Jesus fucking Christ.

Taking my suit jacket off, I reach back to hand it to her, but she just stares at me with a fire in her eyes that wasn't there before.

She's not going to give in and accept my offer, so I toss it to her. I can respect her distrust of me. She has no reason to trust me, and she shouldn't.

CHAPTER 3
Angela

Shoving my arms into the coat thrown at me, I tuck my knees to my chest and wrap the suit jacket around me entirely.

I hate him.

Whoever he is, I hate him.

I have no doubt that my father killed his. My father is a tyrant who barks out orders and takes what he wants, whatever the consequence.

Ducking my chin to my chest, I inhale the manly scent imbedded in the fabric of the coat, and hate how much I love it. His expensive cologne reminds me of the warm summer sun mixed with the faintest hint of something else that I can't place. And it's that spicy/smokey something else that has me taking deeper and deeper breaths, my body having no choice but to relax under the comforting spell of my captor's scent.

I have no idea where we're going, but I know it's somewhere in the city. Manhattan, I think, based on the buildings and architecture I recognize from pictures.

We eventually pull into an underground garage and my heart rate spikes. Lifting his jacket to my nose, I inhale deeply, relaxing all over again, until I look out the window and see my father being dragged from the trunk of another SUV and across the garage.

"Oh my God," I whisper, not wanting to draw attention to myself. I've never seen my father look so helpless, and a deep part of me likes seeing him that way. For once, in this moment, I'm not afraid of him.

"I've got her," my captor says to the man who's clearly in charge beside him. "Then I'll meet you down there."

Down there? Down where?

The tension in the car skyrockets. "You have a lot to explain," the man says, making me shiver as he climbs out.

There's one more man in the car with us, but he remains silent, only throwing me a quick glance before exiting too, giving nothing away in his dark eyes.

My captor takes a breath and then climbs out of the car. He comes around to open the trunk and our eyes lock for a long moment. My head spins with the intensity of his gaze mixed with the intoxicating scent of his jacket that's enveloping me. It's a confusing combination that has my heart racing in both fear and fascination.

gives his finger print while looking into the eye scanner.

The car starts to ascend, and I find the courage to ask tentatively, "Where are you taking me?"

"To my apartment," he says curtly.

"What? Why?"

His back stiffens, but he doesn't answer me. Instead, I watch the numbers rise as we ride in strained silence.

Why would he bring me to his home?

What does he think is going to happen there?

Slight panic starts to set in and I have to control my breathing or I'll give away my nerves.

The elevator stops and the doors slide open, but I make no move to leave the corner.

"Let's go," he commands, holding his arm out to prevent the doors from closing again. When I still don't move, he pins me with a hard stare that makes my heart stutter and knees lock. "Let's go. I have shit to take care of."

"My father?"

"Yes," he grinds out.

"What are you going to do to him?"

"Things an innocent like you shouldn't know about."

I scoff, and his eyes narrow. "You don't know me," I tell him, raising my chin defiantly. "And you can do whatever you want to my father. I know he deserves it."

Surprise flashes through his eyes and he lets his arm fall as he steps right up to me, his presence crowding me.

"You think he deserves what my family and I are going to do to him?"

Beat him, torture him, shoot him. Whatever they do, he

deserves it. "Yes."

"Why?" His dark eyes search mine. "What did he do to you?" he asks in a softer tone, as if it'll make me confess everything to him.

"I don't know you. And I don't share my personal business with those who have kidnapped me."

His already dark eyes turn stormy and he steps even closer, giving me a fraction of an inch of breathing room. "Who the fuck kidnapped you before?"

"I never said I was."

"It was implied."

"What? You want to be the first and only to do that? You'll be disappointed on that front in many ways," I fire back, finding a resilience in me I didn't think I possessed any longer.

Looking away from his eyes that see too much, I slip past him and walk right out of the elevator.

He walks past me without another word to open the only door in the short hallway, and I look behind me at the open elevator doors. But he quickly squashes any thoughts I had of escaping. "You won't make it there before me. And even if you did, it won't go anywhere without my command."

Sighing, I seal my immediate fate and walk inside his house in the sky, my eyes widening at the view of the city lights through the floor to ceiling windows that make up the wall across the living room from me.

"This way." Grabbing my bicep, he leads me down a hallway, and after passing a few closed doors, he opens the next one and gently pushes me inside, switching the lights on.

I turn to look at him, crossing my arms over my chest. "Why won't you tell me who you are?" His eyes burn into mine for a long few seconds, and I see the battle in them. "I think I deserve to know the name of the man who took me."

"I'll be the judge of what you deserve." He turns to leave, but pauses as he's closing the door behind him. I think he's about to say something else, but then he shakes his head and slams the door closed.

I manage to make it to the bed before my knees buckle and I collapse onto it, inhaling the collar of the suit jacket I'm clinging to as the only lifeline I have in keeping myself sane.

CHAPTER 4
Luca

What the fuck is wrong with me?

Why did I bring her up here? I should've taken her down to the basement. I shouldn't care if she's comfortable. I shouldn't care that if I took her to the basement then everyone would look at her and want her for themselves.

My blood is fucking boiling right now. For both the fact that I took Angela and that she's getting under my skin.

She thinks she deserves to know who I am?

What does she even know about the life?

We try and keep the women in our family out of the business and knowing what it is we do exactly, but they always figure it out at some point. They know the life they live isn't normal.

My younger sister, Katarina, has always been kept safe in the family house on Staten Island, and she only just recently turned twenty-two. It's not safe for her. It never will be. Women are always the first target and bargaining chip used when one of our enemies are looking for leverage on us.

Something tells me Angela has been used as a bargaining chip more than once for her family, and that makes me want to put a bullet in Joey's brain even more than I did before for allowing her to be put in danger.

Fuck.

I hate the protective instincts she's evoking in me, and I hate that I want to walk back in there and find out what her lips taste like instead of thinking about how her father is down in the basement right now, ready for a little Carfano revenge.

Locking my place up tight, I activate all of the security cameras so I can check in on her and know if she tries to leave. She'll find it's futile if she does.

Our family owns this building. Leo has the entirety of the top floor and I have the one below him. The floor beneath me is the medical suite, equipped with a surgical room, x-ray machine, recovery rooms, and a bunch of other shit that means we don't have to go to a hospital if something happens. The floors below that are apartments for the rest of the family, guests, and our most trusted soldiers. Then there's a floor of offices and a conference room for family business, and the floor below that is where we have the offices of our legitimate businesses. Appearances are everything. Especially when it comes to the government poking around in our shit.

With a special passcode, fingerprint, and retinal scan, the elevator descends to the basement. It's been converted into a gym with weights, a boxing ring, an MMA cage, and grappling mats where we work on our hand-to-hand combat skills. Past the gym, there's a shooting range with a fully stocked artillery, knife throwing blocks, a meeting room, and our interrogation cells. Those are just four cement walls with a metal chair and a drain in the center of the floor.

As I walk down the hall that opens up to the gym area, I find my brothers and family gathered around the mats with Joey Cicariello on his knees before them. Leo and Alec hear my approach first and turn to give me hard looks.

"What the fuck were you thinking? Where is she?" Leo barks, walking up to me.

"In one of my guest rooms."

His eyes widen a fraction, but he quickly covers his surprise. "In your home? What the fuck are you thinking, Luca?"

"She's locked up tight up there, don't worry."

"That's not what I'm worried about. Why did you take her? Where did you even find her?"

"She was locked in a room down the hall from Joey." I rake my hand through my hair, pulling on the ends.

"And?"

"And I thought she'd be good leverage. But from the little she's said to me so far–" I pause, suddenly not wanting to share her personal business. Especially when I think her father did more than just keep her locked away. "She hates him too."

"What?" Alec asks beside him, his surprise evident.

"She told me he deserves whatever we do to him." I shrug.

"I wonder why," Leo says, his brows coming together.

"I plan on finding out."

I see the look in his eyes change, as if he knows my motives. "She's a Cicariello. Don't forget that. Got it?"

I see the warning in his eyes and hear it in his tone. "Yeah, I got it." Her family is the reason ours has two less.

Retaliation is in our blood. We don't let anything go unanswered. We've had families come after us on the business side, trying to cut off our suppliers to make sure construction projects are delayed, or outbid us on a job at the last minute so that they might be able to jump in and take over for us. But we always recover quickly. And trust me when I say that those who fuck with our businesses, we let them live long enough to see that it didn't work, and then we snuff them out like the little nuisance they were.

But coming after us personally? Joey Cicariello was the first to make that bold move, and believe me, no one will ever make that mistake again.

"You took my daughter," Joey says, a stupid little grin on his face. "Have fun with her. Now that I'm here, she's no good to me."

"What the fuck does that mean?" I growl out, low and menacing, and Leo grabs my arm, holding me back.

"Unless you're willing to let me live if I give her to you"– he laughs, then coughs–"then do whatever you want with her."

"That's your fucking daughter." Leo releases my arm, giving me his silent permission to do what we've all wanted to for a long fucking time.

I reach Joey in two strides, my right fist connecting with his jaw instantly, the snapping back of his head and sound of bone crunching the most satisfying thing in the world right now.

Coughing, he spits out blood in front of him and laughs up at me. "I see she's gotten to you. What kind of bullshit is she trying to tell you about me?"

"Why?" I taunt. "Worried she'll reveal your dark secrets?" Grabbing the collar of his shirt, I send him a warning only he can hear. "I will find out everything, you worthless piece of shit. Then that cocky little grin will turn to real fear and no one will be able to save you. You'll beg for mercy that won't ever come." Pulling back, I see the mask he was wearing slip, and I grin triumphantly. "I see you're getting it."

Releasing him, I back away, and my phone beeps in a pattern that's unique to my security system. I pull it out of my pocket and smile at the image of Angela through my cameras trying to open every door and window. She's fucking beautiful. And still in my suit jacket, my dick jumps at the sight. I want to push it from her shoulders and see her pretty little nipples greet me like they did earlier.

We all have the same alarm alert placed on our phones by Stefano, so I know they all heard it.

"I have to go," I tell Leo. "She's trying to leave."

"And you're smiling?" Nico, Leo's right hand asks,

bewildered.

I wipe the grin from my face. "No."

I hear them talking as I walk away, but I don't catch any of it. All I'm focused on is the little hellion in my place. I keep the security camera feed active on my phone and watch her the entire way up, her growing frustration at finding no way out making her even more beautiful. Her cheeks are flushed, her eyes wide and a little crazed, and her teeth are nibbling on her puffy bottom lip.

Fuck, I want to do that.

Slipping my phone in my pocket when I reach my door, I open it to find her pacing by the windows.

"Have fun trying to leave, *mia uccellino?*"

CHAPTER 5
Angela

"Why did you bring me here?" I ask angrily. "What do you want from me?"

"I want to know what your father did to you."

Crossing my arms over my chest, I look out the windows beside me. "Nothing."

"Bullshit," he says, and I swing my eyes right back to his.

"You can't demand answers to questions when you don't even know the consequences that answering them will bring."

He walks towards me and stops a few feet away, giving me my space. "He's down in our basement."

"What do you plan on doing to him?"

"Do you know who your father is?" he asks, ignoring my

question. "Do you know what being a Cicariello means?"

Unfortunately, I do. I learned at an early age what being a Cicariello means. And especially what being Angela Cicariello means.

"I do," I tell him simply, lifting my chin. I've spent countless days and nights wishing I was born into any family other than mine, and wishing my father wasn't a ruthless mafia boss who didn't adhere to any sort of family loyalty other than to himself. My brothers are his heirs, so he tolerates them. But his wife and daughter? Just annoyances and lesser thans.

Nodding, he walks up to the windows and takes a deep breath. Without his penetrating stare, I'm able to take him in wholly. He's older, maybe in his late twenties, and standing there, he looks to have been carved from marble. Unmoving, statuesque, and hard with intense features that I know are not just present in his face, but in what's beneath his suit, too. Every time he moves, I can see his muscles moving under in shirt. And when he lifted me in and out of the trunk, my fear was temporarily replaced with appeal at how strong, yet gentle he was when holding me.

"He killed my father and my uncle five years ago," my captor confesses, this time with more reverence in his tone than when he pinned me up against the wall back when bullets were ringing out below.

"He's a bastard who has always done things for no one other than himself," I tell him as some low form of consolation. I don't know why I feel the need to, though. He's the one who took me, and yet I still manage to give him a sympathetic apology on behalf of my family. "I'm sorry about your family. But I hope you know taking me will do nothing to aide whatever it is you hope to get from him. He doesn't care about me. He doesn't care about anyone but himself."

A range of expressions flit across his face, from curiosity to anger, and everything in between. "We don't want anything from him that we can't just take for ourselves."

I don't know what that means exactly, so I go back to looking out the windows, finding his stare too intense.

Everything about him is too intense.

"What's your name?" I ask softly, needing to know. I don't want to keep calling him my captor in my head.

He doesn't answer me, but I feel his stare burning a hole in the side of my face, so I give in and look back at him.

"Luca Carfano," he finally confesses, and my heart immediately picks up in pace.

Carfano.

I've heard my father and brothers say that name over the years, and I've always found it to roll around beautifully in my head. But I've heard it more and more these past few months when my father and brothers would discuss business in Italian at the table, knowing full-well I couldn't understand them.

"I've heard him mention Carfano many times. I couldn't understand anything else, though. Everyone discussed business in Italian if I, or any house staff, were in earshot."

"You didn't learn Italian?"

"No," I say with more force than necessary. "My

34

schooling was chosen for me." I press my lips together to keep from telling him how I was struck for even asking to take Italian. My father accused me of wanting to learn so I could use it to eavesdrop on him and his men.

"That's a shame. *Allora sapresti cosa sto dicendo e scopriresti quanto ti trovo bella.*"

My skin flushes. I have no idea what he just said, but it felt like velvet brushing against my skin, making every hair stand on end and leaving goosebumps in their wake.

I know he sees the effect on me because his eyes turn molten and his lips turn up in a little smirk.

Looking away, I take a few shallow breaths. He doesn't get to have any more power over me than he already does.

"I'm tired," I declare, turning on my heel. I only make it a few steps though, before Luca grabs my wrist and spins me around to face him.

I meet his gaze with an angry one. "Let go of me," I say through gritted teeth. "You may have taken me, but I'm not yours to do with what you want."

"Is that so?" he challenges, his neutral demeanor turning icy at my defiance.

"You don't own me." I try and pull my arm from his grasp, but he just tightens his grip.

"As far as you're concerned, *uccellino*, I do."

Again, that sentiment rolls from his tongue and my heart flutters against my will, letting me know that I'm feeling the complete opposite of what I want.

"All you did was take me out of one cage and put me in another."

"With a better view."

"Not from where I'm standing," I tell him, meeting his gaze with a hard one of my own.

A slow, predatory smile pulls the corners of his mouth up. "You're not a very good liar, Angela." He must see something in me that solidifies his assumption because his smile grows. And even though it's not friendly in the least, it still makes my insides twist.

I am a good liar. Just not with him, apparently. So, I decide to throw the truth at him. "Lying resulted in punishment. So, unless you plan on using that hand you have on me to hit me with until you think I've learned my lesson…" I trail off, and his face plunders closed, hearing the truth in my words.

I go to pull my arm free from his grasp again, and this time he lets me. Walking quickly back to the room he put me in, I close the door behind me and begin to pace the entire room, trying to get my heart to settle.

I didn't want to reveal anything to him.

I don't want him to think I'm a victim. I don't want him to pity me.

Something in me wants him to see me as a strong woman. A stronger woman than how I view myself on most days.

When my heart rate calms, exhaustion hits me like a freight train, but I can't go to sleep yet. I need to wash this night off of me.

I didn't bother to look around the room after Luca first left me in here. The moment I heard him leave, I ran out and tried to find a way out of here. But now that I know there isn't one other than him letting me out himself, I start to wander around the room.

I find a walk-in closet almost as big as my room back home, completely empty.

Home.

That word gets stuck in my throat as I try and say it out loud. That word has never meant much to me. I only call it home because it's where I lived, but I never felt at home. I never felt the safety, warmth, or comfort one should when they think of home.

I had nowhere else, though. I've only ever had what my father allowed me to have. Which wasn't much.

Taking a deep breath, I close the closet doors and walk over to the other one across the room. When I flip the light switch on, I gasp, blinking a few times to make sure what I'm seeing is real.

A large glass shower that looks big enough to fit ten, and has as many knobs and nozzles on the stone wall, has a rain shower fixture on the ceiling that I know will feel amazing. Next to it is a jacuzzi tub that's big enough for me to get lost in, and all along the opposite wall are shelves of fluffy towels and beauty products, a cosmetic vanity station, and a his and hers vanity with copper vessel sinks that match the other faucets and fixtures in the bathroom.

It's so beautiful. Everything is beautiful.

Closing and locking the door behind me, I run my fingertips over the shiny marble that makes up the vanity, and then shed my clothes. Stepping into the shower, it takes me a moment to figure out the settings, but once I do, hot water comes raining down on me from above.

I close my eyes, leaning against the smooth stones of the wall as the glass fogs from the steam. I'm used to always being on alert and never truly being able to relax, which is why I'm shocked to feel my muscles unwinding right now. I know better than to rely on a locked door for safety.

I don't know who Luca is, but I know I need to stay as far away from him as I can. I'm already feeling too much when he looks at me.

CHAPTER 6
Luca

Taking my seat at the large conference table to the right of Leo, I feel the eyes of my family on me. I know they want to ask me shit, but they know better.

We usually have our big family meetings once a month, where the cousins fly up from Miami and we discuss the month's business in person. But tonight is an exception since we got Joey in our hands and everyone in the family has the right to weigh in on what's next.

"Everyone's here. Let's begin," Leo declares, taking his seat at the head of the table. "Last night went off without a hitch." Then I feel him look at me. "For the most part."

"What am I missing?" Saverio asks, who just got off a

plane from Miami and hasn't been briefed yet. He runs our club and businesses down there alongside our other cousin Matteo.

"Luca took a little souvenir with him last night," Marco informs him.

"What kind of souvenir? Something expensive, I hope." Low laughs travel around the table. "What?"

"That's enough," I say harshly, slamming my fist down on the table. Looking each of my family members in the eye, I land on Saverio's last. "I took Angela Cicariello. She's currently up in one of my guest rooms."

"Seriously?" he scoffs. "Fuck, man. I forgot he had a daughter. How old is she?"

"Nineteen."

"Oh." His eyes light up. Sav is closer in age to her, but I'll be fucking damned if anyone thinks they can have her.

"Let me put this out there for you and everyone," I say, the deadly tone of my voice making his eyes widen. "She's not for any of you."

"Is she for you?" Marco challenges.

"I haven't decided yet," I lie.

I have decided.

Angela Cicariello will be mine.

She can hate me, but she can't deny that fire I saw in her. I don't even want to tame her fire. I want to feel it under my hands, I want it wrapped around me as I'm deep inside her, and I want to turn it around and use it on her.

"You sure about that?"

My eyes turn to slits.

"Enough," Leo barks. "Despite Luca going rogue and disregarding orders, the fact still remains that she could be an innocent who has suffered at the hands of her family. When Luca finds out more, he'll share it. Got it?"

The sound of yeses mumbled around the table has Leo nodding. "Alright, then, on to the main event. Joey is down in the basement. It's been a long, fun five years tearing him and his little empire down," Leo says with a cruel grin. "But it's time to end it, and him. Fear only lasts so long without a demonstration as to what happens when you attempt to take us down. He's going to stay down there for a while to suffer." His face turns stormy. "He's the reason I had to cause Abrianna years of pain."

Everyone nods around the table.

"But we also have to address the new aggressiveness of the Armenians. They've been dropping bodies in our territory for the past couple months, and with everything that went on with Abri, I put it on the back burner. But now it's back front and center."

"How many so far?" Saverio asks.

"Four. They're dumping in remote alleys along the border of our blocks."

"Do we know what they've been up to lately?"

"After they were busted by the feds for their insurance scam a few years ago, they've laid low, sticking to their usual strongarming and extorting businesses for protection money. Then using them to launder their drug and gun money."

"And who are these guys they're killing? And why dump on our streets? What do they have to gain from that?" Matteo asks.

"They're killing their competition. The men are drug dealers from the gangs they're trying to push out of their territory. Dropping them on ours makes it look like we're doing it."

"Which gangs? Are they looking to retaliate?"

"Low level gangs. But this shit can't keep going. And the fact that they think they can do it in the first place pisses me the fuck off. So, starting tomorrow night, we'll be setting up surveillance teams around our boundaries to gather information."

"I'll set up a schedule between teams now," Stefano offers, typing away on his laptop.

As captains, Stefano, Gabriel, and Marco each have their own small army of men they control, and each oversees different subsects of our businesses. From construction, to unions, to finance, to small businesses, and everything in between.

"To start, make one for every night for the next two weeks," Leo tells him.

"Got it." Stef nods. "I have a program that will create a schedule, all I have to do is enter the names. And…" he draws out. "Done. I'll email it to you all now."

"Good. That's all for tonight."

I'd normally stay behind with my brothers to talk some more, but I don't have it in me tonight.

On the ride back up to my apartment, I remove my tie and stuff it in my pocket. I know Angela is in her room, so when I get inside, I pour myself a glass of whiskey and take a seat on the couch.

Pulling up the security feed from earlier, I watch her make herself a quick sandwich for dinner and then retreat just as quickly back to her room so she doesn't run into me, I'm sure.

I need to get her to come out of there on her own. I can't force her, and I won't. She seems to have been forced to do what others have told her her entire life, which means I need another approach.

CHAPTER 7
Angela

I spent all of yesterday in my room, only sneaking out when I knew Luca was gone to run to the kitchen for some food. I don't want to run into him. Well, want isn't exactly the right word. I'm scared is more like it. He stirred something in me that I don't want stirred.

I haven't had a full meal in two days, though, and I'm starving. Sneaking from my room like yesterday, I'm hoping Luca is gone for the day since the only clothes I have to wear are the pajamas I came here in, and I saw how Luca was looking at me when he first found me. It felt like he could see under them.

Tiptoeing my way down the hallway, I make it to the

kitchen and into the fridge without incident. *Thank God.*

Taking out the eggs, cream, and shredded cheese, I look through the cabinets for a small pan and then combine everything for an omelet. Dropping two slices of bread into the toaster, I make myself a cup of coffee and then quickly eat right there at the counter.

I make sure to wash everything I used before heading back into hiding, but the front door flying open stops me in my tracks.

Shit.

But while I think Luca will come striding in, it's an elderly woman with a duffel bag instead, followed by an elderly man with an armful of groceries. How the hell did he get those up here on his own? Peeking around them, I see a man who I know isn't Luca, but is dressed in a perfectly tailored suit just like him, stepping back into the elevator. Just as the doors close, he looks up and sees me, and flashes me a grin that does anything but make me believe he's friendly.

The elderly man goes back out into the hall for the second batch of bags and then gets to work putting it all away while the woman grabs my hand and pulls me to the center of the living room.

"Uhm, what's going on?" I ask, but she doesn't answer. Instead, she takes out a seamstress's measuring tape and lifts my arms, circling my waist with it. "What am I being measured for?" I try asking, but she doesn't respond again. "Ma'am?"

She fires off a rapid string of Italian and looks up at me with sharp brown eyes.

"I'm sorry, I don't understand."

She makes a tsking sound of disproval and then continues to measure me in every which way possible.

The man she came in with finishes putting the groceries away and walks over, placing a gentle kiss on the cheek of who I assume is his wife. She smiles, murmuring something in Italian to him, and then he's slipping right out the door like a ghost.

She says something else to me, but when she sees I don't understand, she sighs, handing me the bag she walked in with and then following her husband out.

Confused, I open it and see it's filled with clothes. "Thank you!" I yell after her as she closes the door behind her.

Walking back to my room, I dump the contents out on the bed, and after a shower, I put on a pair of yoga pants and a t-shirt. There are also leggings, tank tops, more t-shirts, bras, and panties. I'm surprised Luca even thought about providing me with clothes, and I wonder why that woman was here to measure me if she already had this bag for me.

Shaking it off, I hang the clothes in the closet and climb back in bed, picking up the remote for the TV.

My eyes grow heavy after a few hours of a mindless reality show, and the next thing I know, I'm waking up to a dark room and my stomach grumbling.

Damn it. I should've grabbed some of the food that man brought today before locking myself in here.

Maybe Luca isn't back yet? I don't know what his role in the family is, but he could be away and I'm hiding in here for nothing.

Taking a deep breath, I unlock the door and open it a crack, the scent of something delicious wafting up at me straight away. Looking down, I see a tray right outside my door, and I hesitate for only a moment before taking it inside and locking the door again.

Lifting the silver domed lid covering the dish, I bite back a groan at the sight of a bowl of bowtie pasta in what looks to be vodka sauce with a breaded chicken cutlet and steamed broccoli on top.

Luca left this for me?

I doubt he cooked it, but still…

It's still hot, too, which means it hasn't been here long and he's probably still out there in the kitchen or living room eating dinner himself.

Bringing the tray back up on the bed with me, I dig into what has to be the best meal I've had in quite some time. I finish the entire thing and have zero shame in that.

Stuffed, I put the tray on the floor by the bed and lay back down to watch a few more episodes.

* * * *

I'm startled awake by a knock at the door, my heart practically jumping into my throat. I pull the comforter up to my chin and shove Luca's suit jacket further under my pillow so it's out of sight. I kept it as a comfort. But that doesn't mean I want him to know that.

When I make sure it's hidden, I slide out of bed and

approach the door cautiously.

There's another knock, and I jump. "Yes?" I call out tentatively, placing my hand on the knob.

A string of Italian responds and I relax. It's just the lady from yesterday.

Opening the door for her, she pushes her way in, clearly annoyed that I kept her waiting. She wheels in a rack of clothes and goes straight for the closet.

"What's all this?"

I stand there in confusion until she says something in Italian and quite literally pushes me out into the hall where there are more racks of garment bags, hiding whatever clothes are inside.

Why are there so many?

I don't realize I'm just standing there staring at them with an open mouth until she pushes me some more and points in the direction of the living room.

Huffing out a breath, I do as she wishes and leave her alone to do her work. That doesn't stop me from pacing the living room, though.

Why did Luca have her bring me what seems to be a whole damn wardrobe?

How long does he plan on keeping me here?

My breathing becomes shallow and I finally sit, taking in deep breaths to relax myself. I've watched a lot of videos on breathing exercises over the years to aide in keeping my panic attacks at bay, and so I close my eyes and visualize myself on the coast of Italy, drinking a glass of wine and eating a massive bowl of pasta.

With my next inhale, I breathe in visions of a happier future, and on my exhale, I breathe out the negative energy trying to take over every aspect of my being.

I can't give in and give up. Not when I can almost taste the freedom just outside of this building.

The woman eventually finishes and starts to wheel the racks out the front door where the same man in the suit from yesterday is waiting to help her.

He smirks at me again, and instead of letting it go, I stand and march to the door where he promptly blocks my path.

"Where do you think you're going?"

"Anywhere but here," I tell him. "I don't know why Luca brought me here, but I want to leave. Now."

He flashes me a grin. "That's not for you or me to decide, sweetheart. You're under Luca's protection, so what he says, I do."

"And what did he tell you to do?"

"Help Mrs. G with whatever she needs and make sure you don't leave."

"Is that all?"

"Pretty much." He shrugs. "There were a few things thrown in there about what he'll do to me if I let you go or if something happens, but"–he shrugs–"I don't think I'll have to worry about that, will I?" he challenges, and I meet his stare with a hard one of my own.

I know I can't leave without the help of Luca or one of his men, so I'm choosing to save my battle for another day when I'm more likely to succeed in escaping.

"No. I'll be good," I say, flashing him a sweet smile that catches him off guard. "For now," I add, walking back to the couch.

Mrs. G, as I now know her to be, says something to the man watching me, and he relays the message. "She said that she hopes you enjoy the new clothes and to tell Luca if you need anything else."

"Tell her I say thank you."

Nodding, he does as I say, and the little old lady gives me the first warm look in two days, coming over to kiss both of my cheeks before leaving. With the click of the door closing, I hear the lock slip back into place and I jump up, running straight for my room.

"Oh my God," I breathe.

The closet is filled from wall-to-wall and floor-to-ceiling with everything from comfy loungewear to fancy floor length dresses.

Does Luca really believe I'll need all of this?

The audacity of him.

My fingers brush over the beads of one of the dresses and my anger flares. As if I'd go anywhere with him where I'd need to wear a dress like this.

My panic comes back full-force and I have to lie down, closing my eyes when the room begins to spin.

I breathe until I find myself floating on a cloud, letting it carry me to sleep. I wake again when the sun is setting, feeling much better.

I have to remain strong if I'm going to survive whatever lies ahead. Like right now. I'm not going to cower away from him if he's out there. I'm hungry and I want to make something that brings me the comfort I so desperately need right now.

The only reprieve I used to have back home was learning how to cook with my mother. She taught me every Italian dish she knew, passed down through generations. It was the only place I ever saw her with a genuine smile.

My heart pangs with grief.

She was the only good thing I had in that house. When she passed, there was nothing but darkness that awaited me, and I stopped cooking.

I spot a loaf of bread that's fresh from a bakery and my mouth waters. I pull out two slices and then the cheese and butter from the fridge. My mom and I used to play music while we cooked, but since I don't have any way to do that here, I start to hum the first one that comes to mind as I make myself a grilled cheese. It's not some fancy dish, but it's something my mom and I used to make when we were feeling under the weather, and it always made us feel better.

When it's time to flip the sandwich, I pat the perfectly browned side and pop my hip against the counter beside the stove.

"What song is that?"

Startled, I jump and turn around, finding Luca standing at the edge of the kitchen, leaning against the wall that leads to another part of the house. I had no idea he was even here.

I haven't seen him since the night he brought me here, and the onslaught of how beautifully dark and handsome he is hits me square in the chest. But it's not just that. His presence puts me on edge. My body wages a war on wanting to get closer to him and wanting to run in the opposite direction. Which is why I've tried to avoid him at all costs.

He pushes off the wall and I hold the spatula out in front of me like a weapon, making him smirk, his eyes darting between mine and the utensil.

"Are you going to use that on me, *mia uccellino*?"

"If I have to."

"You'd have to be quick. But I think you should use it on your dinner before it burns."

Realizing how ridiculous I probably look, I pull my shoulders back and turn back to my sandwich.

I reach up into the cabinet above me for a plate, but Luca is suddenly right there, nudging my hand aside and grabbing the plate for me. A cloud of his scent fills my nose and I get dizzy for a moment.

Luca holds the plate out, and in my unnerved state, I think he's trying to poach my grilled cheese, so I slide it onto the plate and turn back to make myself another one. He stops me. "What are you doing? Here." He holds the plate out for me to take. "I was just getting you a plate. I wasn't stealing your food," he says harshly, making me flinch.

Turning the stove off, I try and make a hasty getaway to my room, but he stops me once again.

"Stop," he commands, and my body reacts instantly, freezing on the spot. "Sit at the table."

I take a breath and turn towards him slowly, my anger burning me from the inside out. *How dare he.*

"Did you just order me like a dog to stop and sit?"

"If that's how you want to see it," he says casually, like my anger amuses him. "But I have to talk to you about something."

I stare at him for a beat longer, and my curiosity wins out over my anger, so I take a seat at the dining room table, taking a small bite of my sandwich.

Luca takes the seat beside me, his closeness knotting my stomach so much that I put the sandwich down, unable to even swallow another bite.

"Have you found everything you need?" he asks.

"What I need is to leave."

"And go where?"

"Anywhere else."

"You want to go back to Long Island?"

"No," I say forcefully.

"So, not anywhere else, then."

I narrow my eyes. Is he serious?

"Don't look at me like that. You said anywhere but here. If not your home on Long Island where I suspect you spent most of your days locked in your room, then how about in the basement in a cell right beside your father?"

"He's in a cell?" I ask, my interest piqued.

"Yes." He smirks. "And I see you like that?"

Looking away for a moment, I pick at the crust of my sandwich.

"Hey," he says in a gentler tone, his deep voice vibrating through me and forcing my eyes back up to his. "You don't have to be shy about it. I know hatred and the need for revenge well. I've lived it most of my life. First with my own father, and then with yours for killing my father." Luca's eyes grow serious. "What I'm saying, is that you don't have to hold back from me. You can talk to me."

"Talk to you?" I balk. "I can talk to you? What do you want me to say to the man who stole me away in the night and brought me to this place that has security as tight as a naval base? I'm supposed to trust you? You sent a woman I can't communicate with to supply me with an entire wardrobe like I'm going to be your permanent prisoner. I'm locked in here with nothing but my own company. My life wasn't much before, but I had books. I had music. I was taking classes."

Luca just sits and watches me while I rant on, the words leaving me faster than I can even register what I'm revealing.

"You could've told me what you need."

"Prisoners are allowed to make requests? I'm not supposed to just stare at the wall?"

"Keep it up and you will." Standing abruptly, Luca walks off down the hall he popped out from earlier, leaving me alone with my cold grilled cheese. He goes from one emotion to another so quickly, I'm going to get whiplash. I don't understand how he can be angry, then gentle, then understanding, and then angry again in the span of a few minutes.

Throwing out my sandwich, I place my plate in the dishwasher and head back to my room.

I guess this is all my life is going to be from now on. Just going from prison to prison and never having a say in how and where I live my life.

CHAPTER 8
Angela

Sitting straight up, I gasp for air, my hand coming to my neck as my throat closes on a scream that I catch before it escapes.

I search the shadows of my room, my heart rate feeling like thunder pounding inside my body.

There's nothing there, though. And as the lightning outside flashes, illuminating my room for the briefest of seconds, I see nothing other than what's supposed to be there.

There's nothing and no one but me.

I force a few deep breaths and my throat loosens, allowing me to take slow, deliberate breaths until my panic subsides.

Throwing the comforter off of me, I swing my legs over the side and the cool air of the room hits my damp skin, making me shiver. I reach for the hair tie I left on the side table and throw my hair up into a bun.

My skin is crawling with the sensation that someone else's hands were all over me, and my legs feel like jelly as I walk to the bathroom. All I can think about is soaking in the jacuzzi tub.

Switching the light on, I close my eyes at the sudden brightness, only to open them again and see my worst nightmare standing in the corner, a sinister grin on his face.

He takes a step towards me and my vision blurs with tears, my throat burning with the need to scream, but nothing comes out.

This isn't supposed to happen to me here.

Why did Luca let him in?

Does he know?

Is he in on it?

He keeps walking towards me, his face twisting into something demonic, and I succumb to the blackness I was hovering on the edge of, knowing I can't fight it off.

"Angela!" Someone calls my name from the distance, and I want to go to it. It sounds like heaven calling.

"ANGELA!" The voice is getting closer. I try and go to it, but I'm shaking. I can't fight off the weight holding me under the blanket of darkness.

"ANGELA! WAKE THE FUCK UP!" The voice is right in my ear now and my eyes fly open, immediately locking with Luca's above me.

My ears are ringing from his screams, until I see that his mouth is closed, and I realize it's me who's screaming. My throat is raw and swollen as I suck in ragged breaths, my eyes darting all around.

"Relax," he says in a tight voice. "You're okay, Angela."

"Don't touch me," I say desperately, my voice cracking, and he releases my shoulders immediately. I know he was just holding me down because I was flailing in my sleep, but I can't stand the touch of anyone right now.

Kicking the comforter off, I push him away and run to the bathroom, my knees colliding with the tiled floor just in time for my stomach to roll and the entire contents inside of it to empty into the toilet.

There was enough light coming from the bedside table lamp for me to find the toilet, but when Luca follows me inside and flips the light on, another scream leaves my already raw throat as my eyes immediately go to the corner where I saw *him* in my dream.

There's no one.

He's not here.

None of them are here.

It was just a nightmare.

I scream again when I feel fingers brushing my hair away from my neck. "It's just me," Luca says softly, gathering my hair in his hands.

"Please," I whisper, huddling closer to the toilet.

"What do you need?"

"Please," I whisper again, pinching my eyes closed. I

don't even know what I'm begging for. For him to leave me alone, or for him to help me?

I've already emptied my stomach, but I start to dry heave when the thunder outside rumbles. No wonder the nightmares came back.

Luca lets my hair fall down my back again and I hear him leave me. "No," I panic, but he's back in a moment, tying my hair at the nape of my neck loosely and then pressing a cool washcloth to my heated skin. He dabs at the sides of my neck, cheeks, and forehead, and then lifts my hair to drape it around my neck.

My mind is still in fractures from the vivid dream, and my arms and legs feel heavy. I try to make a move to stand, but I can't. I don't have the energy.

"I've got you, *mia uccellino*," Luca murmurs in my ear, lifting me into his arms.

"Wait," I croak. "My mouth." He seems to understand what I need, so he sits me on the counter and grabs a paper cup from the cabinet below. Filling it with cold water from the sink, he holds it up to my lips and I take it with shaking hands.

Once I've rinsed my mouth out, Luca takes the cup and fills it with a little mouth wash, and I eagerly take that as well.

I don't have the strength to look him in the eyes. I don't have the strength to thank him. I don't have the strength for anything right now.

Taking me in his arms again, Luca shuts the light off and carries me back to bed. Laying me down gently, he covers me in the top sheet only, the cool fabric feeling nice against my sensitive skin.

He flicks the bedside lamp off and I find myself begging him in a weak voice again, "Please."

"I'm not leaving," he assures me, sliding into bed beside me.

I curl into myself, but he pulls me back against his rock-solid frame, caging me within his strength and sheltering me from anything that might try and invade my mind again. But the only thoughts I have right now are of my captor who just brought me back from the depths of my mind that I wish would stay buried.

And I know I shouldn't, but I feel safe in his arms as I succumb to the heaviness surrounding me.

CHAPTER 9

Luca

What the fuck just happened?

I was awoken by Angela screaming. The thick wall separating our rooms did nothing to mute her terrified screams. For a split second, I thought that someone had somehow gotten in my house and was attacking her. I quickly grabbed my key to her door, knowing she always keeps it locked, and what I saw before me was something out of a fucking movie. The psychological ones that fuck with your mind.

Angela was struggling, her body contorting as her arms and legs kicked and punched under the comforter. Her screams pierced my ears and made my fucking chest ache, knowing she was suffering with something I couldn't fight off myself.

When I was finally able to get her awake, she looked so vulnerable. Her eyes were straight portals to the pain she's constantly hiding from.

Holding her in my arms now, she settles against me, and her breathing evens out.

She fits perfectly.

At first glance, you'd think Angela was meek and innocent with her youth and delicate features. But she's far from it.

I need to know what happened to her.

I need to know what made her scream bloody fucking murder like that.

The thought that someone put that fear in her has my blood raging with the need to inflict pain.

But first, I need to gain her trust.

She may have let me take care of her just now, but I have little doubt that when she wakes up, she won't push me away.

She probably thinks it was easy for me to leave her alone for the past few days. Little does she know, I spent every fucking day watching her through my security feed. I would wake up and leave early to go down to my office on our business floor instead of my office here, and I wouldn't return until I knew she was locked away in her room for the night.

I knew she needed space, but that doesn't mean I had the restraint to not watch her. I don't have cameras in any of the bedrooms, but I do have them around the rest of my place. Cameras only I have access to. Stefano does too, as a precaution in case something ever happened to me, but I have a setting that will let me know if anyone other than myself logs into the feed.

The first day when she left her room, I watched as she tiptoed down the hall, her back ramrod straight and her eyes darting everywhere. She was on high alert, as if something or someone was going to pop out at her.

She only left her room to go to the kitchen, but I saw how she looked longingly out at the city below from my wall of windows. It must be a change from her view back on that compound, seeing people going about their everyday lives.

She'll never be one of them.

She'll never have the freedoms they have.

She was born into a life and world that doesn't allow for what everyone else would consider normal.

She's a *uccellino*, a little bird sheltered and kept away from the world where nothing and no one can touch her.

But she's been more than just sheltered. She's been a captive in her home her entire life, and I have a feeling those walls hold more secrets than my family ever knew.

The more I watched Angela, the more I wanted to know every little thing about her. Seeing Mrs. G measuring her in the living room yesterday made my fucking day. She looked so uncomfortable and confused, and yet so fucking beautiful. I want her to be comfortable here. I told Mrs. G to give her a full wardrobe, and I guess that entailed more than I thought, since Angela was in such distress over what having so much meant.

I don't give a shit about the money if that's what she's concerned about.

Watching her made it hard to stay away, but I knew I needed to. And after tonight, I know I won't be able to stay away any longer.

Breathing in her hair, a sense of calm washes over me.

She's the daughter of my enemy, and yet the first thing I wanted to do when I heard her scream and saw her in pain, was help her.

Does this happen a lot?

How often has she woken up screaming and no one was there to help her? Or worse, who *was* there?

My jaw clenches at that thought and I take a deep breath, her scent bringing me back. I tighten my arm around her and she sighs in her sleep, her small hand moving to cover mine on her stomach.

I'm not going back to sleep. I have to make sure I'm ready to bring her right back to the present if her nightmares return. But at some point, I must've dozed off, because I'm startled awake by her trying to pry my arm away from her.

"What're you doing, *uccellino*?" I rasp in her ear, and she immediately stills.

"Why are you in bed with me?" she asks, her voice filled with panic.

"You wanted me to stay with you."

"What?" she shrieks softly, making her cough. Her throat has to be sore and raw from screaming.

"Do you remember what happened?"

She flinches, and since she's turned away from me, I can't see her reaction. I need to see her eyes.

Turning her towards me, she struggles, but I keep my arm strong around her. And with my other, I lift her chin so she'll look at me, but Angela pinches her eyes closed.

"Look at me." She shakes her head. "Look at me," I repeat, putting more authority behind it. "I need to see you."

She hesitates, but then her long black lashes flutter open, revealing the most beautiful eyes in the fucking world. The golden honey surrounding their black center is melting before my eyes, trapping me inside.

Every defense she had up is no longer there, and I can see every emotion as she feels it. She's fearful. Whether it's because of her nightmare or because I'm here in bed with her, I'm not sure. But behind that fear, I see something else. And the longer I look, the more I recognize it as desire.

She's fighting it.

Just like she's fighting her fear, she's fighting wanting me this close to her and seeing more than she wants me to.

"Do you remember what happened?" Angela swallows hard and nods. "How often do you have nightmares?"

She opens her mouth to answer but then closes it, uncertainty flashing in her eyes. "Now it's only when there's a storm."

"Now?"

"It used to be every night."

"Were you always alone when you woke up from them?" The sick part of me wants to be the only one who's gotten to help and comfort her.

"Yes," she whispers, tears gathering in her eyes, making my chest ache. Blinking them away, she looks down, but I tap her chin, and those pots of honey find their way back to mine.

"What happened? What were you dreaming about?"

As open as her eyes were before, they shutter closed and she pushes at my chest. I don't budge.

"Get away from me."

"No."

"Luca. Please," she begs, and at the sound of my name from her lips, I release her.

She scurries away and climbs off the bed. Backing away from me, her eyes remain locked on mine, almost as if they're the only thing keeping her grounded and in the here and now.

"Angela."

"No." Shaking her head, she bolts to the bathroom and slams the door closed. I hear the click of the lock and sigh, scrubbing my hands over my face.

She's going to be more difficult than I thought.

Standing, I walk over to the door and press my ear to it. I don't hear her throwing up, though. If I did, I'd break the fucking door down.

I've never had this protective instinct before.

I want to help her. I want her back in my arms, looking up at me with those eyes that have the capability of making me do just about anything.

I want to see what she'd look like smiling.

I want to see how her eyes would glow if she weren't

haunted and hiding all of the time.

And that's why I was keeping my distance. She has the capability of taking a man like me and ruining him.

CHAPTER 10
Luca

"What have you learned about her?" Leo asks.

"Something happened to her."

"What do you mean?"

"She woke me up last night with her screams." I shake my head, rubbing my jaw. "I've never heard that before. Then when I got in her room, she was fighting with herself. Fuck man, she was scared. I managed to wake her up, but she was shaking, and she ran to the bathroom and threw up. Then this morning, she didn't initially remember that I stayed with her when she woke up."

"You stayed in bed with her?" he asks, eyeing me.

"Yes," I grit. "I couldn't leave her like that. And she

asked me to."

"How is she now?"

"I don't know. She locked herself in the bathroom and refused to come out or talk to me before I came down here."

Leo is quiet for a minute, and I can see the wheels in his brain turning. "Why did you take her, Luca? Why is she in your home? And why do you still have her?"

"I took her because I thought she could give us something on Joey."

"How would she do that? We went there to take Joey, and we got him. We had an agreement with Dom and Geno for Joey, not Angela. They're fucking pissed, Luca."

"I don't care if they're pissed."

His eyes turn black and cold. "You should. Our word is our bond. We're Carfanos, not Cicariellos."

"They won't do jack shit. What are they going to do, come after us? They can't. And they have their weapons back, so they can't use Abrianna as leverage with the Latin Kings."

At the mention of Abrianna, he pushes up and out of his chair, his anger flaring. "You don't know what they'll do. They could keep the weapons for themselves and tell the Latin Kings that we took them and Abri is to blame. What the fuck is wrong with you? You know if anything happens to her–" he cuts himself off, pacing the length of the room.

Abrianna is his fucking world. He would kill me if something happened to her because of my impulsive move. It doesn't matter that I'm his brother.

"Nothing will happen to her."

"You've got that right," he growls. "Dom and Geno

want another meeting. They want her back."

No, is my first thought to that. But Leo is the head of the family. He has no reason to help Angela.

"When?" I clip.

"I told them Sunday. They wanted sooner, but they aren't in a place to demand anything from me. They needed a reminder of who's in control here." Leo studies me. "I'm giving you three days."

"For what?"

He doesn't say anything. He just leans back in his chair and starts sorting through papers on his desk.

He's dismissing me.

Clenching my jaw, I walk out of his office and into mine next door. What the fuck does he mean he's *giving* me three days? Leo always has some plan up his sleeve. It's like he's playing chess, but never tells anyone who's in his game or which piece you are, and only he knows what the outcome will be.

I'm supposed to be going over the reports from our captains on the profits from our gambling dens across the city, but all I can think about is Angela up there in her room with nothing to do. She said she usually reads and takes classes, so I send an email to Stefano with a request, and he immediately replies saying he'll have it done within the hour.

* * * *

I'm fucking tired.

After being up all night with Angela, and then going

through spreadsheets all day, my eyes want to kill me.

Rubbing the bridge of my nose, I step off the elevator and walk the short hall to my door. Opening it, I'm immediately struck with the smell of something fucking amazing.

Angela's not in the kitchen, but I find a note left on the countertop beside the stove under a bottle of olive oil.

Thank you for the Kindle and laptop.

Slipping her note into my pocket, I lift the lid on the pan and groan.

Fuck me.

She made pappardelle pasta in a creamy mushroom and spinach sauce with parmesan cheese crumbled on top. I lift the foil on the dish beside it and my mouth waters at the sight of fresh focaccia with rosemary and cherry tomatoes.

I've watched her make herself simple dishes just for herself these past few days, but now I know *mia uccellino* has been holding out on me.

Knocking on her door, I wait, listening for movement. When I don't hear anything, I knock again, louder.

A few seconds later the lock turns, and she opens the door.

She's only wearing stretchy pants and a loose t-shirt, but her hair is down, hanging wild and free in waves to the tips of her perky tits. Her eyes are wide and clear, framed in thick black lashes that make it seem like she's wearing makeup even though she's not. She doesn't need it. Her skin is clear and smooth, and my hands are begging me to reach out and touch her face to see if she's as soft as she looks. I fist my hands at my sides, resisting.

"You made dinner." I say it as a statement, not a question, and she nods. "Did you eat yet?" I ask, in case she made something else for herself.

"No."

"Come, then." I step aside and motion for her to walk ahead of me. Her eyes widen by a fraction and her grip on the door frame tightens. "Are you afraid to have dinner with me, *uccellino?*"

That gets her attention, and her sharp eyes meet mine, accepting the challenge.

Pulling her shoulders back, Angela steps out into the hall and walks ahead of me. I remain where I am for a moment, staring after her in order to admire the sway in her small hips, my cock stiffening at the sight of her ass in those pants. I want to press her up against the wall and rip them down so I can see if she's wearing anything beneath.

God, the fucking shit I want to do to her is a sin in and of itself. Watching her for days has given me the opportunity to fantasize about every way I'm not supposed to want her.

I'm not supposed to want to kiss, suck, lick, and bite every inch her body before plunging my cock deep into her tight little pussy. I'm not supposed to want to spank her ass red for teasing me in the tight pants she wears every day. I'm not supposed to want to take every ounce of pain and fear she has as my own and let her watch me as I destroy her demons.

But I do. I want all of that. And more.

Following behind her, I watch as she takes out two sets of silverware and places them in front of the same chairs we sat at yesterday while I grab two plates and load them with a helping each of pasta and bread.

Things seem completely different than they did 24 hours ago.

"That's too much for me," she says, eyeing the generous portion.

"You need to eat more. When was the last time you had a full meal?" I ask, eyeing her from head to toe. She's fucking gorgeous. But she'd also be gorgeous with fuller hips I could grab onto, a rounder ass I could play with, and thicker thighs to wrap around my shoulders as she rode my face.

Fuck.

I know she can read my thoughts, too, because her cheeks blossom with a beautiful shade of pink and her little tongue peeks out to wet her bottom lip before she nibbles on it.

Gripping her chin between my thumb and forefinger, I release her lip from her teeth and watch her honey eyes turn molten.

Her breathing becomes shallow, and the gravity pulling me towards her is like nothing I've ever felt. I need to be closer. I need to taste her.

She doesn't say a word and doesn't try and stop me. I still go slow, though. I give her the chance to tell me no, but she doesn't, and I see the desperate need swirling in her eyes, making me want to give her fucking everything.

When I'm close enough to feel her warm breath on my lips, she sighs, closing her eyes – giving me her silent submission.

The only place I'm touching her is her chin, and yet I can feel her body vibrating before mine. *Mia uccellino* is desperate to kiss me. She wants to know what the villain in this story tastes like just as badly as I want to know what the little *principessa* tastes like.

Would her lips singe me with the fire I see in her eyes?

Would they drip with the same honeyed sweetness?

Would they fight me, bend to my will, or give as much as I take?

We hang here in suspended anticipation, and I realize I want to play with my little bird first. I want to give her everything, but I also want to make sure she's ready. I want her to be sure. Fuck, I want her to beg me to give her everything.

I've never had a woman who wanted me – all of me – for more than a good lay or an expensive night out and shit. Don't get me wrong, I was always fine with it, but there comes a point when you want a woman to want you for the man you are and not your bank account or last name.

I'm everything this beautiful little bird should run from.

I'm dangerous.

I'm capable of creating any man's worst nightmare, and do so with a smile.

She deserves someone who will treat her with a kindness she seems to have never known, not a man who wants to fuck her every which way to Sunday, and then some. I want to make her scream in ecstasy, not fear. I want to make her come so hard she forgets where she is and what her name is. I fucking want it all.

I want to be rough, and Angela deserves gentle.

Her warm breath blows across my lips again and I close my eyes for a moment before releasing her chin and taking a step back.

"You didn't answer my question, *mia uccellino.*"

Angela blinks, her glazed eyes turning clear. Her disappointment is evident as she shakes her head gently. "What was the question?"

"I asked when the last time you had a full meal was."

"I don't know." She swallows, looking away. "I was only allowed to eat what was given to me. But it wasn't always like that," she adds quickly. "When my mother was alive, we would cook together every day."

"What happened to her?"

"She died," Angela clips, carrying her plate to the table.

I follow her and sit beside her, this time moving my chair closer so our knees are touching. "How?"

She pushes the pappardelle around her plate with her fork. "There was an accident. She was out walking when a car hit her."

I make sure my doubts aren't outwardly visible for her to see as her big, round eyes find mine. I know what an 'accident' means. There are no accidents in our world. And her mother wouldn't have been out walking by herself and vulnerable for a car to hit her.

"How old were you?"

"Thirteen."

Shit, that's young. And it means she's been alone with her father and brothers and all of their guards for the past six years. The only woman in a house full of men couldn't have been easy.

"After she died, my father started to control everything I did. He always ruled the house with an iron fist, but it was worse after that."

"We're protective of women in this life," I tell her, trying to give her some sort of comfort, but she glares at me with that beautiful fire in her eyes.

"Maybe in your life. Not mine."

"What do you mean?" She's dodged every question I've had about her and her father, but she can't keep it up.

"Nothing," she says quickly, taking a bite of her food.

"Stop doing that."

"What?"

"Stop shutting down every time I ask you about your father or your past."

"I don't talk about it. And I sure as hell am not going to talk about it with you."

"Why not?"

"Because you're just like him. You all are. You'll do anything for more money and more power, and use whoever you need to in order to get what you want. You know what? I'm not hungry anymore," she declares, standing abruptly. I grab her wrist to stop her, and she glare at me. "Let me go."

"Eat."

"I'm not hungry anymore." Twisting her arm, she pulls

free from my grasp, hurrying towards her room to hide from me again. She's always fucking hiding.

Following close behind, I wrap my arm around her waist and spin her to face me, pressing her against the nearest wall.

"You really need to stop running and hiding from me."

"And you need to stop trying to figure me out."

"Not possible," I murmur, running my hand up her hip, then arm, to cup her neck.

Stroking her throat, I feel her swallow hard. "You can run, *mia uccellino*, and you can hide behind a locked door, but you can't hide your reaction to me when I do this." I stroke my thumb over her throat again and her lips separate on an exhale, her cheeks flushing.

Her pulse thrums beneath my hand, the rapid beat a tempo that's calling to the soul I thought I had lost.

"Aren't you tired of hiding?" I goad, wanting her to tell me she wants this. I see her need to let go.

"Yes," she whispers, and I feel her small hands tentatively reach out to rest on my stomach. My muscles contract, her touch singeing me through my shirt. Sliding them up to my chest, she rests them there. "I'm tired of hiding. I'm just so tired of it all."

With my one hand on her neck, I stroke her cheek with the other, her skin just as soft as it looks. It feels like warm satin, and I want to know if the rest of her is just as soft. But that'll have to wait. Right now, I need to know her taste.

"What do you want, Angela?" I ask, needing to hear the words. I need her permission.

"What do *you* want?" she counters.

"I want to kiss you, *mia uccellino*. I want to kiss your lips first, and then every inch of you." Stepping closer, I press my entire body from the waist down against her, letting her feel what she's doing to me. "I want to see your hair splayed out on my pillows and your eyes melting into pools of sweet honey as your pussy does the same on my tongue and then around my cock."

Her pulse races faster under my touch with every dirty thing I confess I want to do to her. She likes it all, which makes my cock swell even more. Angela's eyes widen at the feeling.

It seems my little bird is surprised I want her so fucking badly. Or maybe it's my size pressed against her stomach. I know I'll fit perfectly inside of her, though.

Her breathing becomes short and erratic. "You want a lot of things," she manages to say, breathless.

"I do." I stroke her throat and cheek simultaneously, her breath catching. "Do you want them too?"

The fire in her eyes flares, and her tongue peeks out to wet her bottom lip. I know she doesn't mean for it to drive me even wilder, but my cock jumps, wanting to feel her hot little tongue slide against my length before taking as much of me in her mouth as she can.

I almost forget that I'm waiting for her to answer me, and I lean in closer. "Yes," she sighs, and I close the distance, capturing her lips in a kiss that sends a straight shot of electricity through me.

Her soft, pillowy lips greet mine tentatively at first, then dissolve with mine on a soft moan.

That sound is my breaking point.

Groaning, I dig my fingers into the back of her neck and press my body flush against hers.

Licking the seam of her lips, she moans again, giving me access inside. I slide my tongue against hers and she grips the fabric of my shirt, wanting me closer too.

My blood rushes through me with fucking waves of need.

Need for Angela. Need to be closer. Need to make her mine.

I need everything.

I can tell she doesn't have much experience, but I don't care. She's eager, and that's turning me on more than any woman I've ever kissed. And when she moans into me again, the vibration is a straight shot to my dick.

Taking Angela fucking Cicariello is the best impulsive thing I've ever done.

CHAPTER 11
Angela

Luca kissed me.

I'm kissing Luca.

And I've never felt more alive.

His lips are dragging me from the hell I've been living in and taking me straight to heaven. His body is covering mine, pressing me to the wall and holding me up – shielding me from everything.

Shielding me from the thoughts I don't want to think, from my family, and from my past.

Luca should hate me, and I should want to run as far away from him as I can. But right now, all I want is for this kiss to never end.

I've never been kissed like this, as if I were the air he needed to survive, and I'm dizzy from him taking every ounce I have inside of me.

Tearing his lips away, Luca rests his forehead against mine, our lips still so close together, our ragged breaths shared as one.

"You're full of surprises, *mia uccellino.*"

"How?" I sigh, and I feel his smile's whisper touch against my lips.

"*Sei così innocente eppure mi togli il respiro.*"

"What did you just say?"

He doesn't answer me, instead leans in to nibble on my bottom lip, sucking it between his own. Moaning, my neck arches into his rough touch, trying to get more from him.

I don't know this woman he's made me into. The one I was before he took me never wanted the touch of a man, and yet here I am, every cell inside of me calling to his, to be his.

"Have you gotten your appetite back? Because I'm starving."

"What?" I breathe, my mind not working.

"Dinner, *bella.* Are you hungry?"

"Dinner?"

His dark chuckle has my insides twisting, and he licks my bottom lip in a single swipe. "I'm hungry, and you cooked for us." Pulling back, Luca lifts my chin, making my eyes meet his. His chocolate brown ones are glowing with a ring of gold around their black centers, reminding me of a halo. But I know better than to believe him to be an angel.

He takes a step back and I feel the loss immediately. His

body was a blanket of heat, muscle, and strength I didn't know was humanly possible to possess.

Taking my hand in his larger one, he walks us back to the table, my legs almost giving out the entire way.

I already know Luca Carfano is going to break me in all the ways I haven't already been.

He's going to break me in the way I can't recover from.

He's going to break the last pieces of myself I didn't even know could be broken, but I feel it now. I feel the want and need from my heart and soul to be taken and claimed by this man who holds the key to my survival and the key to my freedom.

He had a laptop and kindle delivered to me today, and I almost cried. I yelled at him and pushed him away, but he still listened and chose to make me more comfortable here. That's why I decided to make him dinner. I didn't think I could get the words out to him, so I thought showing him, like he did with the gifts, was better.

Luca eats a forkful and mumbles something in Italian under his breath. "This tastes like my ma's cooking."

"I'll take the compliment."

"You should," he says, and I look away, my cheeks feeling hot. No one's complimented me on my cooking since my mother. She always told me that a good meal can fix anything.

When I eat as much as I can and Luca is finished, I take our plates to the kitchen and load them in the dishwasher. Putting the leftovers in the fridge, I blow out a frustrated breath and grab a bottle of water, needing to find a way to make an exit to my room without a repeat of earlier. I want it to happen again too badly, which means I need to make sure it doesn't. But when I turn around, Luca is right there, leaning against the island counter.

"I'll see you tomorrow," he says, reaching out to brush the backs of his fingers down my cheek. "Sleep well, *mia uccellino.*"

I manage to give him a small nod, my throat closing around the lump forming.

My feet somehow carry me down the hall to my room and I climb right in bed, not wanting to wash away the feeling of him on me just yet. Closing my eyes, I can still feel his hands on my neck and face. He only touched me there, but it felt like he was caressing every inch of me.

He's probably used to women who are experienced and can give him what he needs because they already know what that is, but I still want it to happen again.

In the dark and under the blankets, I can admit to myself that I want him without shame.

CHAPTER 12
Luca

Angela was never even mine to take, and yet all I can think about is unravelling her thread by thread until her complicated tapestry is fully mine to sew back together.

She tasted like heaven, and I know for a fact heaven doesn't exist for a man like me. If I can have a piece of it for myself while I'm still alive, I'm going to try and hold onto it. And for whatever fucked-up reason, the universe gave me a piece of heaven in Angela Cicariello.

I know she's going to try and hide from me after what happened last night, but I'm not going to let her.

After making a cup of coffee, I head to my office down the hall instead of going downstairs to go over the last of the spreadsheets before forwarding the final report to Leo.

Prior to his death, my uncle Sal ran Atlantic City and our family's casino, The Ace's. He expanded his high-stakes backroom games to all across New York City, using our legitimate businesses to host the events so the Wall Street assholes and CEOs felt more comfortable throwing their money around rather than slumming it in some back alley.

The Cicariellos wanted that when they killed him and my father, but Leo and Alec were ready to step into their predecessor's role. Leo for our father, and Alec for our uncle.

Alec's older than me, which means he should've been underboss, but he always preferred AC to New York. He gets to run the whole fucking city, which plays better to him than being Leo's second in command. I don't want to lead my own city and I don't want to lead the whole family, but having power is in my blood, and I still get to wield it in my position. I fucking love it.

Checking the security cameras, I see Angela sitting on the couch with her Kindle and a cup of coffee, and I watch her for a few minutes. She's not hiding in her room.

I wonder what she's reading, because at one point, she puts her mug down and starts twirling her hair around her finger and biting her lip. Is *mia uccellino* reading a dirty book?

Making my way into the kitchen and through to the living room, she hasn't noticed me yet, so I peer over her shoulder and read for a few seconds, my cock getting hard when I see she really is reading a dirty book.

"Do you want that done to you?" I ask low and rough in her ear. She gasps and drops her device. "Because I can promise you the real thing is better." Her breathing becomes shallow. "Have you ever had a man spread you out on the kitchen counter and eat you for lunch?"

"No," she breathes, and I move her hair over her shoulder, exposing her slender neck. Leaning in close from behind, I run my nose from her shoulder to her ear, breathing her in. She smells like wild flowers, and her chest rises and falls in quick succession.

"Would you like to know what it feels like?" Swirling my tongue around the shell of her ear, I take it between my teeth and she gasps, tilting her head to give me more access. "Instead of reading about it, you could be living it."

Turning her head towards me, I make her look at me, and what I see in her eyes has my dick throbbing with need. But this isn't his time. Right now, I want Angela to feel good. I want her to see that being here doesn't mean she has to be hidden away. I can show her the light.

"Do you want to know what it feels like, Angela?" I ask again, and her eyes flare with desire.

She nods, her little tongue peeking out to wet her bottom lip before biting it.

"I need to hear the words."

"Yes," she sighs, and I capture her lips in a kiss that seals the deal. I'm going to make her feel so fucking good.

Biting her bottom lip, I pull away and round the couch to stand in front of her. "Come." I hold my hand out and she takes it willingly. I pull her up and crush her body to mine, my lips finding hers again.

On her moan, I slip my tongue inside her greedy little

mouth and give her a preview of what I'm going to do to her pussy.

Angela sinks into me and I grab her ass, lifting her up. She wraps her legs around me and I walk us over to the kitchen island and sit her on top, ready to recreate that scene she was reading.

Kissing my way down her neck, I bite her shoulder, making her moan. Fuck, I love that sound.

Lifting her t-shirt up and over her head, I pull the cups of her bra down and swirl my tongue around both of her nipples, making her pant before sucking one deep into my mouth. She cries out, one of her hands going to the back of my head.

Her tits are the perfect size, and I'm already picturing my cock sliding between them as she takes me in her mouth.

Leaving them trussed up from the pulled-down cups, I drag my mouth down her soft, flat stomach, swirling my tongue inside her belly button, making her squirm.

Gripping the waistband of her stretchy pants, I look up at her from between her legs, making sure she's still here with me. Leaning back on her hands, her swollen lips are parted, her eyes are burning amber, and her tits are bouncing and swaying with every shallow breath.

She's a fucking goddess.

"Please," she begs, and I growl. That's the sweetest fucking word she could have said. I like her begging.

Yanking her pants down and off of her, I slide my hands up her legs, her soft, smooth skin like silk beneath my touch.

Fuck me.

I'm going to send Mrs. G a bonus for buying Angela the sexy red lace panties she has on. Gripping them in my fists, I'm able to tear them from her with a simple tug, the delicate fabric no match for my need to taste the candy it's hiding.

I keep my eyes on hers as I slide my hands back down her thighs and grip her behind the knees, spreading her legs wide. The only time I break eye contact is to drop my gaze to see what heaven looks like.

I groan.

She's perfect.

Her pretty little pink pussy is glistening with her arousal, coating her spread lips and giving me all the indication I need that she wants this – me – as badly as I do her.

Blowing cool air on her center, she shudders, a little whimper leaving her lips. "Next time you read that scene, I want you to picture this. Me. You. Us. And I want you to get hot all over and wet with need because you'll be remembering my mouth on you."

Without waiting for a response, I dive in, my tongue licking each of her pussy lips and sucking them into my mouth. Angela's hips buck off the countertop, and I hook her legs over my shoulders as I get to work on my feast.

Her sweet honey melts on my tongue and I groan into her, needing more. Swirling her entrance with the tip of my tongue, I slide it up to her swollen clit that I've left begging for my attention until now.

Angela's legs squeeze my shoulders and lock behind my head, but I don't give her any room to move as I hold her to my face. She's going to take what I give her.

Sucking her clit between my lips, she cries out, her arms finally giving out as she collapses back onto the counter. Every sigh, moan, and cry of pleasure that leaves her makes my cock pulse. He wants to slide into his new home, but not yet. Not right now.

I can feel her shaking beneath me, her body wanting its release, but she's fighting it. Either she doesn't want to let go yet or she can't.

Flicking her tight little bundle of nerves, I scrape my teeth over her clit and she cries out, her hands clawing at the smooth countertop, trying to find something to grab onto.

I know I have her right on the edge, with her pussy leaking more of its sweet honey out onto my tongue like a fucking river. Lapping it up, I slide my hands up her torso to pinch her hardened nipples, rolling them between my fingers and loving the throaty moan torn from her lips as her back arches off the counter.

Everything she does is so fucking beautiful. She's so responsive to everything I do, and not in a fake way to please me. She genuinely can't help herself, and that makes me want her even more.

I'm used to women falling at my feet to please me and to have just one night with me, but this is ten times better – the daughter of my family's number one enemy splayed out on my kitchen island with my face buried between her legs.

With one more teasing spin of my tongue around her entrance, I pinch her nipples hard and plunge my tongue into her hot little hole. Her inner muscles quiver and then clamp down around my tongue in waves of fucking ecstasy.

Angela screams out her release, her sweet honey flooding my mouth. I eagerly drink it up. Every drop she gives me is a gift I earned and fuels me with a power I've never felt running through my body.

Peeling her legs away from behind my head, I look down at my little caged bird who I just saw fly for the first time, and Lord have mercy on my damned soul, I want to watch her fly again, this time with my cock buried deep inside of her.

Lifting her into my arms, she mumbles something inaudible and I carry her down the hall to her room, gently laying her down on the bed. She immediately sighs and curls into herself on her side, facing away from me.

I pull the sheets over her, sorry to cover up the beautiful work of art I just uncovered, when a piece of dark fabric sticking out from under her pillow catches my eye.

Her head is only half on the pillow, so I'm easily able to slip my hand under and pull whatever it is out without disturbing the now sleeping Angela.

What the…?

She has the suit jacket I gave her in the car on the night I took her folded under her pillow. I forgot that I hadn't gotten it back, but I don't understand why it would be under her pillow. Has she been sleeping with it this entire time?

Confused, I stand there for a minute looking between my jacket and her sleeping form. I don't know what's going on in that head of hers, but when she wakes up, I plan on finding out.

CHAPTER 13
Angela

I'm having the best dream. One where Luca has given me a reality better than the book I was reading. I normally don't read such steamy books, but because of Luca, I was curious.

Smiling, I hug the sheet close to my body, and my eyes fly open, suddenly realizing that my dream isn't a dream, but a replaying of what actually happened.

The room is dark now, meaning I've been asleep for a while, but my body flushes with heat at the memory, as if it wasn't hours ago that Luca had his hands and mouth all over me, but merely minutes ago.

I had no idea he was home again this afternoon, but I was sick of being in my room. And after the kiss the night before, I was almost hoping that I would see him again so it could be repeated. Then he snuck up behind me and all bets were off.

Was I picturing Luca doing to me what the male lead in the book was doing to his woman? Yes. But I didn't expect him to be there to give it to me in real life.

It was amazing.

I never knew I could feel like that. Like I was completely out of control. As if I was shot straight into space, my body not my own anymore as it was torn apart until all the pieces floated back together and I drifted down to earth again.

Stretching out, I yawn and roll onto my back, gathering enough energy to climb out of bed and shuffle into the bathroom. I catch a glimpse of myself in the mirror and cringe. My hair is a mess, and the only thing I have on is my bra, oddly enough.

Quickly using the bathroom, I comb out my hair and splash some cold water on my face before redressing in leggings and a light, loose sweater that's longer in the back than the front.

I'm starving, but just as I'm about to leave my room, I catch sight of Luca's jacket draped across the chair in the corner of the room.

Oh, no.

That's the jacket I had folded under my pillow and have slept with every night. His scent has all but faded, but I still find comfort in it somehow.

He probably thinks I'm some freak for having it under my pillow, and now he left it out for me to see that he knows.

Huffing out a deep breath, I run my fingers through my hair and close my eyes, calming my nerves.

Stepping out into the hall, I'm hit with the delicious scent of Chinese food, making my stomach growl on cue.

Luca is in the kitchen, taking out white cardboard boxes of food from a paper bag. He looks up when he hears my approach, and his heated eyes take me in from head to toe and back, making my body flood with need. He has the power to turn me into a puddle of desire with a single look, and I hate him for it. I shouldn't want him the way I do.

Taking a deep breath, I sit at one of the bar stools around the island and feel my cheeks heat when I look at the counter.

When my eyes find his again, I see his little smirk, and know he's thinking the same thing.

"I wasn't sure what you liked, so I ordered everything."

"I haven't had Chinese in years. My father didn't trust take-out. He said it would be easy for someone to tamper with it."

"He's right," Luca says casually. "If he didn't take the proper precautions, that is. Plus, he knew we were after him."

"So, you're not worried someone is trying to kill you and willing to poison your food to do it?"

"Someone always wants us dead, *uccellino*," he says proudly, as if it's a badge of honor. "I always give a fake name when I order and have one of my men pick it up and deliver it to me."

"You've got it all figured out."

"Not everything," he says, looking at me intently. "Some

things are more difficult to figure out."

"Maybe not everything is meant to be figured out."

"Yes, it is."

"So, it goes both ways?" I ask, feeling bold. If he wants to figure me out, then I'm going to need the same from him.

"It can."

"Alright."

"Fine." He nods, handing me a plate.

We each dish out what we want on our plates and then take our seats at the table.

"What do you want to know?" Luca asks, breaking the silence.

"What's your position in the family?"

"Underboss to my brother Leo. He was in the car when I brought you here."

"The mad one."

"He's not exactly thrilled with what I did."

"Me either," I say without thinking, then pinch my lips together.

"You seemed pretty thrilled this afternoon," he practically purrs, his voice dropping to an octave that has my skin rising in goosebumps.

Pushing my Lo Mein around my plate, I take a deep breath before meeting his gaze. His usual chocolate brown eyes have grown darker, boring into mine with an intensity that has me flooding with the need for a repeat of what we did earlier.

"I can see in your eyes that you're thinking about it right now. So am I, *uccellino*. And I can't wait to do it again."

Swallowing hard, I rub my thighs together under the table, trying to get the image of him between my legs out of my mind. But it's all I can see right now, and it's all I can do to not beg him to touch me.

I've never felt this deep seeded *want* before.

I never had the opportunity to.

No one has ever awoken my body like this. Quite the opposite, really.

Luca places one of his large hands on my knee to stop my movements. "I can relieve that ache you're feeling." He squeezes me gently and then rubs circles around my knee, the motion lulling me into a calm stupor that's fogging my brain. "But you'll need to eat first."

"Hmm?" I question, my focus solely on the warmth that's rapidly spreading through me from where he's touching me.

"Eat, Angela. Then I'll take care of you."

Blinking away the fogginess, I see the deep want in him too, and my stomach flutters. This man wants me, and not because he made a deal with my father.

I've only ever had one other person want me despite my father, and it didn't end well for him. My father killed him for trying to help me escape when I was sixteen. A flash of guilt hits me hard and I look away, pushing Luca's hand off of me.

"I don't need taking care of."

"Hey," he says firmly, putting his hand back on my knee. "What happened?"

"What do you mean?"

"What just went through your mind that made you shut

down?"

I clear my throat. "Nothing."

"Tell me. I don't like seeing that look on your face." He begins to slowly rub circles around my knee again, and I'm lulled right back under his spell.

"I was just thinking about someone in my past. He tried to help me, and it didn't end well."

"What made you think of him now?"

"You. The look in your eyes." I pause, taking a deep breath. "But it doesn't matter right now."

"You can tell me," he urges, but I shake my head.

"No. Not tonight." Luca studies me for a moment. I don't know what he's seeing, but he drops it for now and goes back to eating, leaving his hand on my knee, though. And I don't shove it away this time. I like the comfort too much.

When we've finished eating, I take our plates and Luca packs up the remaining leftovers.

Closing the fridge, Luca backs me up against the kitchen island and cages me in with his arms on either side of me, gripping the edge of the countertop.

"You know I'll find out everything, *uccellino*. You keep retreating into that beautiful head of yours right when–"

"Right when you try and trick me into talking?" I can't do this with him. He's asking too much of me and pushing me too far. "You're the one who barged into my room and took me against my will. *You* brought me here and *you* seduced me, and now you think that means I'm going to tell you everything about me? You don't know me. You don't know my family. And you certainly don't have the right to demand anything from me. This afternoon was a mistake and won't be happening again."

"That's where you're wrong," he says furiously. "I know you want it to happen again."

"Stop pretending to know me."

"Stop pretending to know *me*. You think I'm just like your father and brothers and everyone else you've ever come in contact with." His eyes are black now, boring into mine like they're trying to drill the truth into me. "But what you don't know is that I'm worse. I can do whatever I want with you here." He leans in closer and my pulse skyrockets, my mouth going dry. "You know I'm right. But I also know that you're more than willing. You just don't want to give in to what you know will be the greatest pleasure of your life. You'd deny yourself that?"

A chill runs through me. He's right, but I refuse to let him know he's winning. If this afternoon was any indication, then sex with him would shatter me. It would be the greatest pleasure I've ever known, but it would break me beyond repair. He'd be indefinitely imprinted on me and in me.

And as much as I want to not want that, I do.

If this is all I'm granted in life – this brief reprieve from my reality – then I want to take advantage of it. I want to have the memories to carry me through whatever comes next. Good memories I can cling to when I have nothing else.

I lift my chin defiantly, refusing to give in weakly. "I never said I was going to deny myself anything,"

His smile blinds me, the predatory nature of it making my insides twist in anticipation for what's to come. He looks like he just trapped the prey he's been circling and playing with for the past few days.

Because he has.

And the fucked-up part is that being his prey feels like an honor. Being wanted by this man feels like I possess a power of my own, and I want to be trapped by him. I want to be at his mercy and the sole focus of his attention.

His dark eyes assess me, holding mine hostage in a gaze that makes my head spin and my body flood with need. The longer he stares, the harder my blood rushes, breaking through my defenses and letting the truth that's lying behind them free.

When he sees this, his eyes flare like I just breathed life into the simmering coals that lie just beneath his surface, creating a fire that's about to be unleashed on me. And I've never wanted to burn so badly before.

His hands dive into my hair and he presses his body flush against mine, searing his lips to mine. Moaning on contact, I grip the fabric at his hips, needing to brace myself on something, anything.

My mind wipes of everything but my need for Luca. He has the power to erase everything that should keep me from wanting him. I need that. To both forget and to feel something other than the numb nothingness I usually do, and the fear and pain on those stormy nights.

Luca's fingers dig into my scalp, holding me to him as his lips imprint with mine. Opening for him, we both moan when our tongues clash in a dance that has him transferring his flames into me, through me, and over me – melting me into a malleable substance he can mold however he pleases.

I'm letting myself be his for as long as I can, because if there's one thing I'm certain of, it's that I'm not meant to have a life with a happy ending.

He bites my bottom lip and then smooths it out with his tongue. "You made your choice, *mia uccellino*," he rasps, roughly gripping my breast and pinching my nipple through my thin bra. "Now you're going to be at my mercy."

I groan, and he cuts me off with another kiss, stealing the air right out of my lungs.

Lifting me up, I wrap my legs around his waist and he carries me through his apartment, never breaking our kiss. Adjusting me to open a door, he kicks it open and storms inside, tossing me down on a bed. I take quick note that we're not in my room based off of the black comforter beneath me, but I don't have the capacity to look anywhere other than Luca.

His jaw flexes as he unbuttons his shirt, and my mouth waters with every inch of skin exposed. Shrugging it from his shoulders, it cascades to the floor in a flourish and I bite my lip, holding in the moan that threatens to escape.

He's so damn beautiful.

Shedding the rest of his clothing, he stands before me, letting me take him in for the briefest of moments before grabbing my ankle and dragging me down the bed towards him. "You're wearing too many clothes."

Luca pulls my yoga pants down in one swift motion,

exposing my skin to the cool air and making me pebble in goosebumps. Sliding his hands up my legs, he leaves a trail of fire in his wake, then quickly strips me of my t-shirt, leaving me in just my panties and bra.

Looking me in the eyes, he licks my lips and kisses his way down my neck and chest, sliding his hands behind me to unclasp my bra, tossing it aside with my shirt.

"*Così fottutamente bella. Non vedo l'ora di divorarti.*"

Luca swirls his tongue around my nipple, sucking it deep into his mouth, making me arch off the bed to get closer to him. His teeth graze my hardened peak and I shudder as he pays equal attention to my other.

I'm panting, every sigh and moan leaving my lips a sound I've never made before. He plants open mouthed kisses down the center of my chest and stomach and drags his hot tongue across the skin right above my panties.

Biting down on the lace, Luca tugs the scrap of fabric down, and I lift my hips to help him in his efforts. When he has my panties around my ankles, he drops them to the floor and kisses his way back up my legs, parting them as he goes.

His mouth settles between my thighs and he takes a deep inhale, closing his eyes and murmuring something in Italian that I don't understand.

Luca's arms bulge beside my head as he braces himself, and I run my hands up them, unable to resist touching his golden skin taut with ropes of muscle.

I can feel the heavy weight of his thick cock on my inner thigh, and I sigh, parting my legs. I wonder what he'll feel like inside of me. I wonder if an orgasm will feel as good with him in me as it did with his mouth on me.

"Luca," I moan, his tongue doing wicked things to my breasts.

"Say it again," he demands, low and rough. When I don't right away, he bites the side of my breast.

Gasping, I moan his name again. "Luca."

"Best thing I've ever heard, *uccellino*," he rasps in my ear. Reaching into the bedside table, he pulls out a small foil packet and rips it open with his teeth. Rising on his knees to roll it down his length, my eyes widen, my nerves suddenly taking hold of me.

I…

"Hey," he urges, gripping my chin so I'll look at him. "Stay here with me."

Nodding, I tentatively reach out and run my fingertips down his chest and abs, his muscles contracting as I do.

Luca grabs both of my wrists and holds them above my head, kissing me hard. Holding my wrists with one of his large hands, he glides his other down the length of my body, settling it between us. He circles my clit with the pad of his finger and then drags it down to my entrance, slowly inserting it inside of me.

"Ohmygod," I say in a rush, pinching my eyes closed.

"Look at me," he demands, and my eyes flash open to his. "You'll keep your eyes on me. Got it?"

"Yes," I choke out.

Luca slides his thick finger in and out of me, sending sparks shooting through my body. "You're so fucking tight," he growls, adding a second finger to stretch me open.

"You're going to strangle me, *uccellino*," he says wickedly, curling his fingers inside of me, stroking my front wall.

I suck in a sharp breath, and Luca's eyes glitter with dark intent, skyrocketing my pulse. Swirling my clit with his thumb, stars burst in front of my eyes when Luca's lips turn up in a grin, and I let go of everything, my orgasm washing over me in waves.

I struggle to keep my eyes open and on Luca's, but I need to. I want him to see me as much as he wants me to see him. And as I sink beneath the waters rushing through me, Luca is right there – right here – to keep me with him.

As the waves subside, Luca releases my wrists and slides his fingers out, replacing them with his cock pressing at my entrance. He pauses, looking down at me. Reaching out, he traces circles and swirls around my stomach and chest, flicking my nipples and then dragging his fingers up my neck to cup my throat entirely.

He doesn't squeeze, just keeps ahold of me, pinning me in place. "I'm not going to be gentle, *uccellino*. I'm going to fuck you until your eyes roll back, and then I'm going to keep fucking you until you pass out from coming so hard."

Entering me in a single thrust, I grip the sheets on either side of me as the breath leaves my lungs. I'm deaf from my pounding blood, but I can hear Luca stringing Italian together in rapid sentences, the beautiful lilt calling my soul to the surface for him to take.

Pulling out of me slower than he entered, his eyes are wild, roaming over every inch of my body as he slams back into me with a force that would push me up the bed if not for his hand around my throat, keeping me in place.

Luca's grunts and growls as he pounds into me make the corners of my lips turn up in a grin I can't control. This man may hold all the power in the world for all I care, but in this moment…under him and at his mercy…I'm the one with the power to make him lose control. I'm the one with the power to make him turn into an animal.

I grip his forearm, sliding my hand down to the wrist he has around my throat. His other hand on my hip tightens in response.

Neither of us needs to utter a word. I see what he needs in his eyes and I want to give it to him. I want to give it to me, too.

Gripping his wrist, I press it down on my throat further. His eyes widen a fraction, then flicker with a devilish pleasure, pleased with my insistence. He takes it as all the permission he needs, and as if a switch is flipped, he snarls, pressing me into the mattress and fucking me even harder. I know I'll feel him still, even when he's not in me and around me, and that has me wanting this even more.

As someone who doesn't feel much other than the monotony of days passing by with only my ghosts keeping me company, I need this. I need to be grounded in the here and now, and I need something drastic to make me feel.

I just want to feel something good.

And as I edge toward the tipping point, I rake my nails down Luca's forearm, needing him to join me in this euphoria I've never known could be possible.

He grinds his hips against mine, sending sparks flying up

my spine and down my legs.

I lift my shaking legs to circle his hips, and cry out at him hitting me at a different angle. And when he grinds against me again, white stars dot my vision. The orgasm I was holding onto hurdles me off the edge and it feels like my heart is going to beat out of my chest as my eyes roll back.

Luca growls like a wild animal, pistoning through my release, the wet slapping sounds of our bodies coming together bringing me back to life. I know he's not done yet. He promised to make me come until I passed out, and I know he's a man of his word.

Finding my strength again, I dig my heels into his firm ass, the sounds leaving me uncontrollable. The look in Luca's eyes feels like he's seeing into me – every part of me – and shoving the demons he knows I live with away with every thrust, sending them deeper and deeper into the recesses of my mind where they can't reach me unless they claw their way back out.

"Let it all go, Angela. Come for me," he demands, and there's no way not to obey. His words seep into my bones, filling my very essence with the need to let go.

My inner walls start to flutter, and he releases my hip to pinch my swollen clit.

I lose it.

My muscles tighten and then loosen as my body follows Luca's directions. I can't stop the tsunami rushing through me, and I don't want to. It destroys everything that has kept me from this kind of pleasure.

Luca stills inside of me, his deep, throaty roar vibrating

around the room and through me, setting off another wave.

I can't keep up with it.

I can't keep my head above the water any longer to watch him let go as he demanded I do.

His dark eyes are the last thing I see and cling to as everything goes black around me.

CHAPTER 14
Luca

She was fucking beautiful.

Amazing.

Ethereal.

Angela may be young, but she's far from naïve. Who would've guessed my little bird would love having my hand around her throat, holding her life in my hands?

She gave me her trust.

She gave me her body to use how I wanted.

And in return, I gave her what I know she truly desires – freedom.

My little bird is passed out in my bed, and I leave her there to rest for now, because I fully intend on fucking her until she can't walk and her pussy is swollen and sore. I'll be imprinted in her. No matter what happens, she'll always feel me and remember that I was inside of her.

Stepping out of the shower, my phone beeps next to the sink and I look to see a string of messages I missed from Leo. Unlocking my screen, I scroll through them.

Fuck. Fuck. FUCK!

Tossing my towel into the basket in the corner, I walk back through my room and into the closet, dressing in black slacks and a black button down. I leave the top few buttons undone and roll my sleeves up.

Running my hands through my still wet hair, I look at Angela asleep in my bed. I can't resist stroking her cheek, needing to feel her soft skin before I go and deal with some shit. She's curled on her side, the curve of her body calling out for me to trace, but I resist, turning on my heel and walking silently out of the room.

I'm tempted to lock her in so she doesn't get any ideas of leaving my bed, but shake my head clear of that thought. I don't know how long I'll be.

When I'm in the hallway and waiting for the elevator, I dial Leo.

"Why didn't you fucking answer me sooner?" he barks.

"I was busy."

He pauses, his silence an indication that he knows exactly what, or who, I was busy with. "Get the fuck down here. You were apparently too busy to catch that someone is stealing from us, too."

"I'm in the elevator," I tell him, and he hangs up.

FUCK!

The entire ride down to the basement, I rack my brain for what could've been off, but I don't recall there even being a red flag for me to second guess something in those reports.

In the basement, I walk through the gym, passing the men who are here getting a late workout in and those training for the fight in a couple weeks. We have a few top contenders.

If there's money to be made, the Carfanos have a stake in the game, both legal and illegal. That includes underground, no holds barred, MMA fights. We hold matches once a month, and everyone comes crawling from the depths of the city to compete. It's by invitation only for the spectators, and we have a truce that's in place inside the facility between everyone present. There's no business disputes or bloodshed other than that spilled in the fights.

The pussy Cicariellos haven't showed for the past five years, but the other four families are all represented – Carfano, Melcciona, Capriglione, and Antonucci. The Irish, Armenians, Bratva, and Yakuza send their best men, too.

Hundreds of thousands, some nights millions, in bets are made depending on who's fighting. But it's a night about more than money. It's pride and power and bragging rights. And my family has all three in spades.

Heading for the conference room, I find Leo and Nico sitting with papers spread out in front of them.

"Who's stealing from us?"

Leo's eyes meet mine in a cold stare that would make anyone other than me piss themselves. I'm used to them.

Grinding my jaw, I bite back what I really want to say, knowing he'd lay me out on my ass in a flash if I did. "What did I miss?"

Leo pushes the papers across the table to me and I go over every line he has marked with a tab.

Fuck.

I go over it again before looking up. His face is unreadable, but Nico's brows are drawn together, thinking.

"The numbers are off. What was cashed in for chips at the beginning of the nights versus what was paid out and what became house money doesn't make sense."

"Exactly. You're lucky I had Nico look over what is supposed to be your job."

"And why did you? You don't trust me?"

"You know I fucking do. I just knew you were otherwise occupied with your new guest and thought the numbers seemed off when I saw a drop in the past two months now."

"I should've caught it," I concede, rubbing my jaw.

"Yes, you should've."

"Who works these two games?"

"Oscar is in charge of them," Nico informs me. "He's being brought over now and Taylor is taking over."

"Taylor's been working under him for years. He could be a part of it too."

"We'll find out. We need him to run the games tonight, though. He'll get the fucking hint after seeing Oscar being escorted out of there."

"He's here," my cousin Gabriel tells us, poking his head inside the conference room.

"Show him to the cell next to Joey," Leo says, then looks back at me. "Do you plan on talking to Joey before she goes back?"

"Goes back?" I grind out. "She's not a pair of fucking shoes to be returned."

Nico smirks. "Sounds like she's a pair of shoes you want to keep."

"She's not a pair of shoes at all, you fucking asshole."

His smirk grows. "Defensive."

I take a deep breath to try and calm myself, not wanting to say anything else that could be turned around on me.

Leo leans back in his chair. "Did you get the information you wanted from her yet?"

"No."

"Do you plan on getting it?"

"Why are you both talking so cryptically?" Nico asks, and I silence him with a look, then answer Leo.

"I do." I just don't know when. I want to know Angela's secrets, but I want her to tell me. I don't want the lies that her father will tell me. "What are the details of Sunday?"

"We're meeting them at Giorgio's at 2."

I nod in agreement. It's our territory, but as neutral as we'll get for a meet-up. Giorgio's is a deli in Brooklyn that makes the best anti-pasta in the city.

"I don't want them here again and we're sure as fuck not going to them. We'll have men do a sweep and then set up around the perimeter and inside by 8 to make sure they're not planning a set-up. And once we know they're not bringing war to our doorstep, we'll make the exchange."

My jaw clenches. "What are we getting in return?"

"Abrianna's safety," he says harshly. "And staying off the radar of the Latin Kings. I don't exactly feel like having to go to war with a street gang who only knows how to spill blood and make noise. We could annihilate them in the blink of an eye, but we don't need the attention. Got it?"

"Of course I've got it. Let's go question Oscar." I stand and round the table to leave, but Leo grabs me before I make it out the door.

"Luca, this has to happen. Do you understand that?"

"Yes," I hiss, pulling my arm free from his grip.

We make our way to the cell next to Joey's, and Leo and I walk in together.

"Why am I in here, Boss?" Oscar asks Leo. His voice doesn't shake, but I can see it in his eyes. He knows exactly why he's here.

"Did you think I wouldn't find out, Oscar?"

"Find out what?"

"Don't play dumb. The only thing worse than playing dumb is thinking you could steal from me and get away with it." Leo walks up to him and crouches in his face. "And it looks like you just checked both boxes."

Oscar's face falls, dropping all pretenses.

"See? So much better when we're all honest. Now, why did you take my money, Oscar? Do I not pay you well?"

Leo pays his men well. Our grandfather taught our father, who taught us, that when you deepen the pockets of your men, their loyalty will run that much deeper. Respect too. Leo may sit on top, but he shares his wealth with everyone. That's how he remains on top.

"I needed more," Oscar admits, diverting his eyes around the room.

"And you couldn't come to me?"

"I…"

"You, what?" Leo clips.

I look down at Oscar and notice that he's shaking, sweating, and his skin looks pale. He's been with the family for a long time, from my father's era, and I've never seen him like this or have ever had a problem with him.

"What're you on, Oscar?" I ask calmly, and his eyes widen.

"Wh-what? N-nothing," he stutters, giving himself away.

Leo grabs Oscar by the collar. "What the fuck, Oscar? Is it coke?" Oscar's eyes are as wide as saucers, and then he looks down in shame, giving himself away again. "Who do you owe money to?"

"Cicariello," he mutters, and Leo pushes away from him, cursing under his breath.

"And you're more scared of not paying them than stealing from me?" he questions with an eerie calmness. "Did you think I would go easy on you because I've known you a long time? Or did you think I wouldn't find out?"

"I don't know."

"You should know I have zero tolerance for thieves and liars. Those who betray the family must pay the consequence."

"Boss, please," he begs. "I'm sorry. I can stop. I can pay you back. I'll work for free. I'll tell you whatever you want to know about Dom and Geno."

"Let's start there."

"Things with Elise aren't going well, the baby won't stop crying, and our son is a fucking nightmare. I just needed an escape."

"What do your family issues have to do with Dom and Geno?"

"I got to talking to one of the high rollers one night a few months ago and he gave me a baggie of blow and a card that got me access to a private club he owns. It spiraled from there. I found a dealer in the club and didn't know he was one of Cicariello's men until I couldn't pay anymore."

Fucking disgusting.

This piece of shit couldn't stand his family so he started getting high and going to a sex club.

"So you decided you were so fucked already that you'd steal from me on top of it all?"

"Yes." Oscar deflates with an invisible weight crushing his shoulders. "I'm sorry, Boss."

"You know I don't accept apologies. And I sure as fuck don't give second chances. You're a sorry excuse of a man to trade your family for pussy and blow."

"You'll find out what it's like," he sneers. "When your bitch starts nagging you about money and seeing the world and that you're never around."

There's a moment of strained silence, and I know what's about to happen a split second before it does.

Leo whips out the gun he keeps holstered under his jacket and fires off a shot, the loud bang echoing around the small cell. Oscar's scream is just as fucking loud, the little pussy. He only shot him in the right shoulder, and the force probably would've knocked him over if the chair wasn't bolted to the floor.

"Speak about my woman like that again and I'll make sure you die a very slow death." Leo presses the barrel of his gun to the wound, making Oscar whimper. "I'll bring you to the brink of death and then bring you back, only to slowly kill you all over again. Is there anything else you want to say about her now?"

Oscar shakes his head.

"My father trusted you when he was alive, and I gave you a chance to prove yourself." Leo steps back and holds his gun a few inches from Oscar's forehead. "You disappointed me." Leo pulls the trigger without remorse, as is expected. We don't give second chances. Once you lose our trust, you lose your life.

"Have this taken care of," he says to Nico, "and let Taylor know I'll be coming to the games next week to talk to him about his new position." He leaves the room, his face devoid of all emotion.

Nico sighs and looks to me. As his right-hand man, he has Leo's ear, but he also has the responsibility to do his bidding. "I'll call in the cleanup crew."

Nodding, I leave him alone with Oscar, whose head is slumped forward with blood dripping down his face onto the floor at his feet.

My place is quiet when I enter, and I walk over to my drink cart and pour myself a finger of whiskey, downing it in one shot. Pouring another, I let the slight burn of the amber liquid spread through my veins.

Stalking down the hall, I unbutton my shirt as I go, and when I step into my room, I can make out her form on my bed.

Good, she stayed put.

Undressing fully, I can't take my eyes off of her. And when my cock springs free of its confinement, I groan, needing to be inside her again. Just thinking about her gets me fucking hard as a rock. And seeing her laying in my bed, imbedding her scent in my sheets, makes me even harder.

I stroke my length.

I don't let women sleep in my bed. I fuck 'em and chuck 'em, their purpose served for however long I need them.

But Angela…

One taste of her and I wanted more. I knew I wouldn't get my fill after just one time. And right now, I plan on filling her up with my cock and having her sweet moans and cries for more fill my ears and echo around the room.

Angela's lying on her stomach, and when I crawl into bed beside her, I trace a single finger down the length of her spine, over her perfect rounded ass, and then the backs of her thighs. Her face is turned away from me, but I hear her sigh in her sleep at my touch.

I make sure I don't disturb her as I place one knee between her thighs, wanting to wake her with my mouth.

I kiss her legs, her ass, the small of her back, and then follow that with the scraping of my teeth over her ass cheeks. She shivers, moaning softly into the pillows.

Gliding my nose along the crack of her ass, I smell her arousal and I bite back a groan. *Mia uccellino* is wet for me and I haven't even gotten started.

Gripping each of her cheeks in my hands, I spread her open and lick her in one long pass, her surprised gasp and then moan bringing me a satisfaction I've never felt before.

"Luca," she moans, and I press my tongue to her clit, wanting to hear her say it again. "Ohmygod," she says in a rush, but it's not what I wanted.

I suck her little nub instead, and then flatten my tongue, the change in pressure making her gasp and then moan, "Luca."

Ah, music to my fucking ears.

Gripping her ass harder, I lift her hips off the bed and push her legs apart with my knee, spreading her wide open. I bury my face in her pussy, her juices coating my nose, lips, and chin – her heady scent filling my senses and driving me to a feral need to have her. To own her.

Angela's cries are muffled by the pillows and I want to hear her loud and clear. Keeping her hips up with my face and one hand on her ass, I reach up and grab her hair, pulling it so her head lifts up. A strangled moan is ripped from her throat, driving me harder.

I release her hair and spread her wide again, lifting her hips higher to give me even greater access to the sweetest fucking pussy in the world.

I've always loved pleasuring women and giving them an experience I know no other man ever will. But this…I can't stop with Angela. I want to give her everything and push her to her limits.

With one more flick of her clit, she starts to shake, and I shove my tongue inside of her, her pussy squeezing around me immediately. Her scream makes my blood sing, and I take every drop of her golden honey as it pours into my waiting mouth.

Her orgasm goes on and on, and when I slide my tongue up to her puckered little hole between her cheeks, I rim the forbidden entrance and she shudders, pushing back into me.

This sexy little minx wants more.

Pressing hard, I breach past her tight halo of muscles just the slightest, and she screams, her body detonating all over again until she goes limp.

I massage her ass, loving that she has enough to fill my hands. Licking the arch of her spine, I move her hair to the side and kiss my way up her neck.

Angela sighs, but her eyes remain closed.

"Sleep well, *mia uccellino*," I whisper in her ear, lying beside her and pulling her close.

My cock is hard between us, but I ignore him. When she recovers, I'll wake her again, this time with my cock spiking through her wet folds.

I can't wait to see her eyes fly open to meet mine when I do.

CHAPTER 15
Angela

I don't know how I got here. To a place where Luca waking me with his mouth on my core is a reality.

When this is over, and when he gets tired of me and is done playing whatever game he's playing with me to get to my father, I know I'm going to still want him.

He woke me up with his mouth in the middle of the night, and then again in the early morning, sliding right into my already wet center.

Carrying me into the bathroom, Luca sits me on the edge of the tub while he turns the shower on.

"Come," he says, and I take his outstretched hand.

I walk under the water raining down from the ceiling and

close my eyes, letting it cascade over me gently. When I open my eyes, Luca is leaning against the wall in front of me, his eyes hooded and his hand gripping himself, sliding it up and down his length.

Oh my God.

My nipples pebble in an instant and the spot between my legs tingles, already needing him there again.

We stare at each other, our eyes roaming down the other's body. When our eyes meet again, something passes between us. Something different.

My eyes drop to his hand on himself, and I watch him pleasure himself, the tingling between my thighs turning into a rhythmic pounding.

I go about washing my hair, and he never takes his eyes off me, nor I him.

This seems too intimate. More intimate than him inside of me, even.

His eyes on me make me feel beautiful in a way I've never seen myself before. Beautiful in a way that's more than what I see in the mirror. Which is good, because what lies underneath isn't all that pretty.

Luca continues to fist himself, and feeling bold, I squeeze body wash into my hand and run my hands up my arms and over my chest, cupping my breasts. Luca grunts, his hand tightening on himself.

"Pinch your nipples," he orders, and I do as he says, rubbing my tight buds with my sudsy fingers. "Lower." Sliding my hands down my hips and across my stomach, I run them down the lengths of my legs, and when I straighten again, Luca's eyes have turned to slits. I give him a small smile, the power I feel giving me the confidence to tease him.

I add more body wash to my hands and then dance my fingers across my lower stomach. Luca's hand starts working harder, and I glide my finger through my slit, rubbing circles around my clit. Biting my lip, I moan softly, my legs already starting to shake.

"Inside of you," he growls, and I slide my fingers down to my entrance and easily slip them inside as far as I can in my standing position.

"Ohhh," I moan, moving them in and out of me.

I need more though.

I go back to massaging my clit, and with my eyes on Luca's, I find my release at the same time he does, our groans echoing off the tiles and glass.

I almost fall to my knees, but Luca reaches out and wraps his arm around my waist, hauling me against his body to keep me up.

Capturing my lips with his, my skin prickles with the little sparks that make me realize I'm in trouble with this man. And that scares me.

Rinsing off, Luca steps out and grabs a towel from the shelf and pats me dry before wrapping it around me.

"Thank you," I whisper, and he nods, grabbing a towel and drying himself off too.

While Luca goes into his closet, I leave his room and go next door to mine. Opening the lingerie drawer, I pull out a matching pink satin bra and panties set. They feel so luxurious against my skin. I've never had such elegant and classy undergarments before. I was allowed to order clothes and such back home, but it was always opened first by one of my father's men to ensure I truly was just ordering clothes.

It was so embarrassing. I tried to only order bras and panties when it was absolutely necessary. I would see the look in the eyes of whichever man had to bring me my packages, and I hated it. It felt like he was imagining me in them from that moment onward, and all I wanted to do was disappear in that house. Which is hard to do considering I was the only girl besides the cook and housekeepers.

Shaking off those memories, I find a matching pink silk robe and cinch the tie around my waist. I don't feel like putting on clothes just yet.

Tying my wet hair up into a bun, I slide my feet into a pair of fuzzy slippers and head to the kitchen. I may have hated the fact that the woman who measured me gave me an entire wardrobe, but I can't fault her on her choices.

I'm feeling adventurous this morning, so I decide to make banana walnut French toast with cinnamon butter, scrambled eggs, and bacon. I even find a French press in one of the cabinets along with a fancy bag of coffee to use instead of the Keurig.

While the coffee is steeping, I contemplate whether or not I should tell Luca. Whatever just happened in the shower changed something between us. The lines are beginning to blur in whatever we're supposed to be.

But not thinking too much past the fact that I made extra and I don't want it to get cold or go to waste, I go in search of him.

He must have left while I was changing because he doesn't answer when I knock on his room door. I pause for a moment, deciding if I should go looking for him on the other side of the apartment. But it's decided for me when I walk back into the living room and find him standing there against the wall by the kitchen like last time.

"Oh," I gasp. "I was just looking for you."

"I know." He smirks. "That's why I came to you."

"You know?"

"I have cameras, *uccellino*."

"You do?" I croak, then realize what he's saying. "You've been watching me?"

"Of course," he says matter-of-factly, as if I should've known that. "Do you think I would've left you alone here without knowing what you were up to?"

"Are there… Are there cameras in my room?"

He tilts his head to the side, a little smile playing on his lips. "No. There aren't any in the bedrooms." The way he says 'bedrooms' is like a purr, and I feel it caress my skin, images of us in his room flitting through my mind. "No matter how much I wanted to see you those first few days."

"Good," I say, crossing my arms. "I made breakfast. We should eat before it gets cold." Walking over to the island, I press the pump down on the French press and bring it over to the table I already set.

After the first bite, Luca moans. "Holy shit, this is fucking good."

Pride swells in me at pleasing him. "Thank you."

"Your mom taught you well."

"She was amazing." I smile weakly, sipping my coffee. "I know she protected me from most things growing up. It could've been much worse. I know that now."

"What did she protect you from?"

"My father. His business."

"Angela," he starts, but I cut him off.

"No," I say curtly, cutting into my French toast with more vigor than necessary.

"You can go see him today if you want."

"Why would I want to do that?"

"You seem to have a few things you need to work out with him before he's–" he cuts himself off this time, and I furrow my brows, unsure of why until it hits me.

"Dead," I finish for him, and he nods, drinking his coffee. "How long do I have? Why is he even still alive?" Luca's face shuts down and I quickly add, "Forget I asked. I know not to ask."

"You can ask. I just may not answer. If you want to talk to him, you need to do it today."

I swallow hard, giving him a small nod.

I try and summon some sort of emotion in regards to the knowledge that my father will be dead soon, but I don't have any. I'm sure as hell not sad. But I'm also not happy either. I'm neutral. Indifferent. For all intents and purposes, he's been dead to me for years.

I can't look at Luca. "I'll think about it."

"You don't have to. It was just an offer."

Standing, I pick my plate up and walk into the kitchen.

"Angela," he says right behind me, startling me. I didn't

hear his approach, and the plate I had in my hands clamors to the counter. He places his hands on my hips and spins me around, pinning me against the counter. "Look at me." I try to fight it, but my eyes find their way up to his. "You don't need to see your father ever again if you don't want to. Okay?"

"Okay," I whisper.

"And you don't need to feel bad about what's coming, either."

How does he know?

"I can see it in your eyes, *mia uccellino*." He presses his body closer to mine, making my head spin.

"See what?"

"That you want him to be punished and don't care what happens to him." Cupping my cheek, he rubs his thumb back and forth, lulling me further under his control. "You look innocent and small, but you're not. And that dark piece of you you're afraid to show on the outside that actually wants your father to suffer before he's killed…I find it incredibly fucking sexy."

He slides his hand on my hip up my back and then down to cup my ass over the robe, his eyes flaring. "You're not wearing any clothes under here."

"I am. Go ahead and check for yourself," I challenge.

Licking his lips, my eyes follow the path of his tongue as it swipes across his lower lip, wishing it were on mine. His fingers pinch the bottom hem of my robe and raise it up, skirting them along the bottom curve of my butt cheeks. I shiver at his light touch, goosebumps fanning out across my skin.

The pads of his fingers run along the seams of the silk panties that cut into my cheeks and expose the bottom half. Slipping them underneath, he presses his fingers into my meaty flesh, pulling me closer.

"Your ass is barely covered," he rasps, pulling the front tie of the robe loose to part the delicate fabric. He takes a step back to get a better look. "*Bellissima*," he whispers, running a single finger along the mounds of my breasts above the lace edging of the cups.

Luca takes in the entire length of my body, his eyes feeling like a warm hug.

"You call this wearing clothes?"

"I'm covered, aren't I?"

"Barely." Sliding his finger down the center of my breasts and stomach, he dips it beneath the waistband of the front of my panties. "You can't look this delicious and expect me not to touch you." With his eyes locked on mine, his hand disappears inside my panties, cupping my entire center and slipping his thick finger inside of me without warning.

Gasping, I sway forward and grip his shirt tightly.

"Already wet," he muses. "Is this for me?" He already knows the answer to that question though.

"Yes," I sigh, his finger slowly moving in and out of me.

"You were sitting there while we ate, wearing next to nothing, your sweet little pussy slick with need. For me."

"Yes," I sigh again, and his eyes flare.

Luca's other hand cups my breast, pinching my hard nipple through the thin satin and lace fabric.

It's a straight shot of lightning to my core and my pussy floods with fresh need as he continues to slowly work his finger inside of me.

"More," I beg, clenching around his finger, making him grunt. He gives me what I want, adding a second finger and stretching them apart inside of me before curling them against my front wall. I choke on a moan and collapse back against the counter.

Luca continues to play me like a finely tuned instrument, fully at his mercy. "You're not allowed to come yet, *mia uccellino*. If you're going to tease me with this little outfit of yours, then you should fully expect to get fucked up against the nearest wall or on the closest surface."

I bite my lip, trying not to lose myself. His words shouldn't excite me the way they do, but the image of what he's saying flashes in my mind and I can't help but want that. I'll take whatever he wants to offer me like a junkie needing my next fix. I won't ask questions and I won't put up a fight.

"Do you understand?" he asks roughly, twisting his fingers inside of me and on my nipple, the jolt of pain making me cry out.

My legs start to shake. I can't last much longer.

"Answer me, Angela," he demands, the authority in his voice rolling through me and bringing me closer to the edge.

"Yes," I'm able to choke out, "but I need to."

"Not yet," he growls, pulling his fingers from me and releasing my breast in an instant.

"No!" I cry out, hitting his chest. He only smiles cruelly, knowing he has me right where he wants me.

"I told you,"–he leans in, licking the shell of my ear–
"you're not allowed to come until I say you can." Pulling
back, I meet his intense gaze, the dark brown of his eyes
melting into pools of chocolate I want to swim in. "Today,
you're going to be mine. I want you to give yourself to me
completely. I won't hold back, and neither will you."

"I didn't know you were holding back."

He smirks, and my chest tightens. "You haven't gotten
all of me yet, Angela."

A shiver racks my spine. I'm dizzy.

I've been battling the feelings I've started to have
towards Luca, ashamed that I feel anything at all. But a night
where it doesn't matter who he and I are to each other, or
how we got here…

Nervous butterflies take flight in my stomach, replaced
with the deep desire and need to be taken by the man in front
of me.

Leaning up on my toes so I'm closer to his lips, I grip
the back of his neck. "Starting now?"

Luca's mouth slams down on mine, his lips hot and
demanding, making every inhibition I have dissolve into a
puddle at our feet, leaving just the raw and real me. The me
I've never been able to be, and the me I don't think I'll ever
be again.

Luca gets it – gets me. He understands where I came
from, and knows that there is no saving me from the fate I
was dealt.

But for a brief moment, I can shed it all and be the girl
who believes she can be saved, and believes she can have it

all, even if just for a day.

His hands are everywhere. And everywhere he touches me, he leaves his mark. An invisible web spun around every inch of my flesh.

Gripping my ass, he lifts me up and I wrap my legs around him, my hips grinding against his, trying to find any relief I can. I slide my hands through his short hair, with just enough for me to grip at the back of his head. And when I close my fists around the ends, he groans into me, the deep vibrations making my core throb harder.

I'm so caught up in him that I don't even notice that we're in his room until he's tossing me down on the bed.

"You're so eager, *uccellino*." No words will form, so I just nod.

Luca sheds his clothes, and when he's towering over me, naked from the waist up with his broad chest and shoulders on display, I squeeze my thighs together.

He's beautiful.

He's dangerous.

He's dark.

He's sexy.

And he's looking down at me like he finds me just as beautiful, dangerous, dark, and sexy.

Unbuckling his belt, he flicks the button of his pants open and slides the zipper down, all the while keeping his eyes on me. He's watching my reaction.

My eyes move down his tanned, toned abs, and stay locked on his hands as he pushes his pants to the floor. His cock springs free – long, thick, and hard. I want to feel its weight in my hands. I want to know what it would feel like to have him in my mouth, and know what he tastes like.

"Sit up," he commands, and I quickly do as he says, which puts his cock right in front of me. "Take me in your hand." I reach out and brush my fingers down his length. "Fist me," he growls, and I see the satisfaction at my instant obeying flit across his face.

He runs the backs of his fingers from my temple to my jaw in a caress that has me wanting to please him even more.

"Open wide, *mia uccellino.*"

Opening my body to him is one thing, but taking him in my mouth is entirely different. It's the shift in power. I have the ability to bring him a pleasure he can't get by himself.

I swirl my tongue around the swollen head of his cock, the moisture that's already leaked from him coating my tastebuds. I didn't know what to expect, but it wasn't this. As if his essence is contained in his come, I feel it run through me, giving me some of his power and domination.

I need more.

Sucking the entire head into my mouth, Luca grunts, sliding his hand through my hair to grip the back of my head.

Our eyes are locked on one another. I couldn't look away if I wanted to. I'm lost in them.

I take as much of him in my mouth as I can manage and then pull back, swirling my tongue around him.

"Grip me harder."

I take him again, and then glide my fist up and down the rest of the way. I soon find a rhythm, and his hand tightens on the back of my head, the bite of pain flaring the throbbing of my clit.

"Enough," he says gruffly, pushing me away. He leaves my mouth with a pop, and I fall back onto my elbows. "I'm not coming unless it's inside of you."

My knees fall to my sides and his nostrils flare.

"I can see how wet you are." Luca slides his hands up my calves and inner thighs. "You're soaked through." Leaning down, he licks me through my panties, sucking on the fabric. "Mmm, you taste so fucking sweet. I want to keep teasing you and make you wait, but I don't think I can. I plan on taking you every way I've fantasized."

"Please," I sigh, spreading myself wider.

"I like hearing you beg." He smirks. "Maybe I'll make you do it a little bit longer."

"No!"

"Yes." He flashes me a grin that makes my heart rate jump. It's as close to a smile as he's given me and it's magnificent. I'd endure anything for another one.

Pushing the silk robe from my shoulders, Luca reaches around my back and unclasps my bra, pulling the straps down my arms along with the robe.

"Perfetto. Sei Perfetto."

I don't need to know Italian to know what he just said, and my heart flutters.

Sliding his hands up my sides, he circles my nipples with his hot tongue, purposefully avoiding the stiff peaks.

"Please," I moan, arching off the bed, trying to get him to give me what I want.

I feel his lips curve against my skin as he kisses his way

down my stomach. Holding my legs open with his large hands on my inner thighs, Luca runs his tongue along the waistband of my panties, then the seams along my inner thighs. He's so close to where I need him, but still so far away.

"Luca." I huff, gripping his hair. "Please," I beg, not ashamed in the least. "I need more."

"The word please coming from your lips is almost as sweet as the way you taste. *Ti darò di più, mia uccellino. Molto di più.*" Blowing cool air against my soaked panties, a chill runs down my spine, flooding my panties even more.

"Luca," I moan, and he flashes me another victorious grin, making my chest twist.

Gripping my panties, the delicate fabric easily tears in his fist and his nostrils flare as he inhales sharply. "This is all mine," he murmurs to himself.

Grabbing a little foil packet from his pants on the floor, Luca tears it open with his teeth and then rolls the condom down his length. I watch him intently. The sight of him touching himself, even to just put a condom on, is so incredibly sexy.

Pushing me up the bed, Luca crawls over me, his heavy, rigid cock grazing my leg along the way. With a long pass of his tongue up my throat, he bites my chin.

"I'm going to fuck you so hard, your pussy will be bruised and you'll feel me every time you move."

"Please," I beg one last time, knowing it's what he needs from me.

His lips crash against mine and he enters me in a single

thrust, pushing me up the bed at the force. We both groan. I wrap my arms around his neck, but he takes them away and pins them above my head. Holding me down, Luca pistons into me. I feel every slam resonate through me like the hard bass of a rock song.

He's going so deep.

He's stretching me so wide.

I'm at his mercy as he fulfills his promise. He's giving me everything, and I know I'm going to feel him inside of me for days to come.

All I hear is the wet slapping of our bodies coming together and my moans filling my ears.

Wrapping my legs around his hips, Luca growls while I cry out. He goes even deeper. He grips my wrists tighter and somehow finds a way to go even faster and harder.

My orgasm builds in me like a tsunami – the tide pulling back, creating a bigger and bigger wave. When it reaches its crest, and I'm reaching my tipping point, Luca knows, growling at the feel of my inner muscles fluttering around him.

"Not until I say."

Crying out, I claw at his biceps. "Please," I beg shamelessly.

His eyes are holding mine hostage, watching me with such an intensity, it feels like he can see straight to my soul.

I want him to see me, too.

I want him to see the damage I've been built upon and stitch every broken piece back together until I can look at my reflection and see a whole person again.

"Come. Now," he commands, and the wave inside of me crests and breaks, pummeling down through me. I ride the wave, giving into it and letting it take me to the utter depths of my soul, the euphoric absolution letting me float back to the surface and back to Luca, his roar of release clearing the fog I had over me.

I don't even realize the ringing in my ears is from my screams until Luca captures my lips, swallowing my sounds and keeping them as his.

Releasing my wrists, I feel the heaviness start to pull me under straight away. And when he pulls out of me, I whimper at the loss, feeling empty without him inside of me.

Luca leaves me for a brief moment, and when he returns, he lifts me up and pulls the sheets back before placing me down and covering me.

"Rest for now, *mia uccellino*," he says, pulling me against him. "Because we're nowhere near done."

CHAPTER 16
Luca

I need her again.

Angela passed out a half hour ago, and I've stayed awake, listening to her breathing and feeling her heart beat through my hand I have resting on her rib cage.

I told her we'd have today, and that wasn't a lie. I just didn't tell her I meant we *only* had today.

This is me being the selfish bastard that I am, wanting this. For once in my goddamn life, I'm giving in to a luxury in life I can't afford to keep for the long haul – her.

I don't look women in the eyes when I fuck them. I don't want to memorize every inch of their bodies and which places get what reaction when I touch, kiss, lick, or bite them.

I don't want to hear their pleas, cries, and moans for more on a loop in my head to replay over and over even when they're not around. I don't want to take their orgasms and wear them as fucking badges of honor for any and everyone to see so they know who's fucking her right.

But with Angela, I do.

I've spent my life stringing together one-night stands, but I want more with her.

I know she's still hiding something from me, but even still, I want to protect her. I want to keep her as my little bird because she makes me *feel* something I don't understand.

I want more time to figure it out, but I don't have time, and I don't want to waste the time I do have.

I need her again.

My cock didn't even go soft. Not with all the ways I want to take her running through my mind. Having her at my mercy, beneath me and spread wide, is an image I'll be pulling out to use after tomorrow.

Kissing the side of her neck, I graze my teeth across the top of her shoulder, and she sighs in her sleep. Pulling the sheet down to her waist, her nipples tighten into hard peaks that I tweak between my fingers.

Angela moans, pushing her ass back into me, her cheeks nestled around my cock.

Fuck.

Sliding my hand down her stomach, I easily slip my fingers through her wet folds and groan, pressing down on her clit.

She gasps, her body stiffening and then melting back

into me. "Luca," she moans, my cock twitching at the sound of my name falling from her lips

"Good, you're awake," I rasp in her ear, pushing her onto her stomach. Throwing the sheets off of us, run my fingers down her back and over her ass, kneading her cheeks and murmuring, "Your ass is perfect. It would be even more perfect reddened with my hand, don't you think?" Her groan as a response sends fire racing through me, and when my palm connects with her ass, the slight jiggle and instant reddening of her skin breaks something loose inside of me.

I slap her ass, alternating between both cheeks. Watching the blood rush to the surface brings a satisfaction to my blackened soul. I love seeing her squirm and hearing her gasp and moan with every connection.

Lifting her hips up so she's on her knees with her ass high in the air, I spread her knees apart and groan when I see her juices coating her pretty pink pussy and leaking down her inner thighs.

"You liked that," I muse, massaging her cheeks, then slap one again. "Didn't you?"

"Yes!" she cries out, gripping the pillows in front of her.

Aligning myself at her entrance, I rub the tip of my cock through her slickness. "How about this?" I ask, entering her in one swift motion, sheathing myself in her heat.

Fuck, she's tight. She's strangling me with her hot, silken pussy, and I remain here for a moment, until her muscles squeeze around me and I can't hold back any longer.

I pull out of her slowly, and seeing my cock coated in her juices, I realize I forgot to put a condom on. But I can't stop. I couldn't stop even if the building was on fire.

I never fuck without a condom, but my mind and common sense are lost when it comes to Angela.

She's too young, beautiful, and innocent for all the filthy shit I want to do to her. But that doesn't mean I'm not going to. It's too late for that.

Pounding into her, I know there's no coming back from this – from her.

She grips the pillows harder, and every time I slam into her, she cries out. But I want to hear her scream.

Reaching around her, I pinch her clit and she detonates, her raw scream sending fire down my spine. Pulling out, I fist my cock that's dripping with her come and pump myself twice before shooting my load all over her lower back and ass.

Angela collapses to the bed. My come glistens on her smooth skin and I swipe my finger through it, using it to write my name down her spine.

"Did you just write your name on me?" she mumbles.

"Yes. I want you to sleep with me on you."

"Mhmm," she hums in agreement.

My chest tightens. If I could slow down time so tomorrow doesn't come for another week, or year, I would.

But tomorrow has to happen.

This is all I'm allowed in this life.

Family. Duty. Honor. Respect.

It's the Carfano way of life. What I want doesn't always matter.

CHAPTER 17
Angela

When I finally wake up on Sunday, the bright light of the sun is streaming in through the sides and crack in the blackout curtains. Stretching out in Luca's bed, I find I'm alone and curl back into the comforter. His scent is everywhere, and I inhale it, letting it calm me.

He never brought up finding his jacket under my pillow, and I'm grateful for that. I'm too afraid to know what he thought anyhow.

Yesterday was something else for me. Luca is nothing like I thought when he first busted into my room. I was fearful for my life and safety. But right now, while I'm warm in his bed, it's hard for me to recall or recreate those same feelings. All I'm feeling is satisfied, and it's a feeling I didn't realize I could have after all this time and after…everything.

I thought I'd need gentle, but he knew differently.

Luca was rough, dirty, and borderline demeaning. And I loved every second of it.

It should be wrong to want him to spank me until my ass hurts, but I didn't want him to stop. I was dripping wet and my ass was on fire, and I still needed more. I still craved more.

His dominance wasn't scary, his forcefulness didn't make me want to be anywhere but right where I was, and the pain rode the line right along with the pleasure, heightening my nerve endings so every touch felt like a lightning strike to my core.

Rolling onto my back, I wince, biting back a groan. I'm sore, and my core throbs at the memory.

I can still feel him all over and in me. Luca made good on another promise. He gave me himself yesterday. All day and all night. I don't even know how my body was able to keep up with him, but I did. And I gave him everything in return like he wanted.

My eyes flit to the bedside clock and I gasp. It's already 11:30. I haven't slept in in I don't know how long. I never had that luxury. Father said breakfast was at eight or you didn't eat. I always had to be up, dressed, and deemed presentable for the day should anyone see me. He didn't want me to embarrass him.

Climbing out of bed, I use his bathroom and then wrap a towel from his shelf around me so I can sneak on over to my room to shower and get dressed.

I feel lighter somehow, and I find myself humming as I walk down the hall, smelling coffee. But when the hall opens up into the living room, I stop short. There are two men here. One I recognize as his older brother, Leo, from the car that night I was taken, standing with a mug of coffee in the kitchen. But the other, the one sitting on the couch with a newspaper, I don't recognize. He's massive and scary, with a scar running down his jawline, looking like he could kill me with a flick of his wrist.

My palms get clammy. Why are they here? Where's Luca?

Something's happening.

I try and back away quietly so they don't notice my arrival, but as soon as I take a step back, the scary one's head snaps up, his eyes locking with mine.

I can feel the evil seeping off of him, filling the air with a tainted thick cloud that leaves a bitter taste in my mouth.

Why would Luca let him in here?

"Boss," he grunts out, and Leo's head turns towards me. With the both of them looking at me, their eyes assessing me, I steel my spine and don't give them the satisfaction of cowering away like I'm sure they're used to.

"Angela Cicariello," Leo states, his voice carrying a note of question. "Luca shouldn't have taken you."

My eyes narrow instinctively, but I keep my mouth shut out of respect.

He looks at his watch. "You have an hour to change and be ready."

"For what?" I ask softly, my mouth dry.

"Has Luca not told you?" I shake my head no. "Today's the day you go back home."

My stomach drops.

No.

I can't go back there.

I don't *want* to go back there.

"Luca's sending me back? Where is he?"

"He's busy right now." Leo's voice is low and commanding, carrying with it an authority that no one but him as a boss could possess. It runs through his veins.

"But he…" I trail off, last night replaying through my head. "I thought…"

"You were never his to take. And you were never his to keep."

His harsh words hit me square in the chest, the reality of my situation twisting my heart to where I have to rub the spot over it to get it to beat again.

Leo and the other guy watch my every move.

I'm so stupid.

So fucking stupid.

My feet find a way to move, and I run back to my room. But it was never mine. It was just another cage.

Tears threaten to form, but I blink them away and take a few deep breaths. He doesn't get the satisfaction of making me cry. None of them do.

It's my fault anyhow.

I let him in. I let myself think that Luca wanting me meant he wanted more than just sex from me.

But no.

That's all men ever want and all I'm apparently good for.

Ripping the jeans and t-shirt I had on off, I put on what I know they expect of me. They expect me to play the good little mafia girl, and so I'll give it to them. I'll let them think that's who I am. But I'll find a way out of this. I'll find a way to finally be free. I'm so sick of being pulled in the direction others want me to go in, and I refuse to live that way for the rest of my life.

If there's one thing I know no one expects of me, it's to escape.

Walking into the closet, I pull out the perfect outfit to play the naïve, sheltered, and demure nineteen-year-old everyone seems to believe me to be. But I'm also the daughter of a ruthless mob boss, and while I hate him, his blood still flows through my veins.

I can play games. I can pretend.

I pull out a cream colored, knee-length, fit-and-flare dress with cap sleeves that's made of a soft, thick material. I add a thin burgundy belt at the waist before the skirt flares out, and pair it with burgundy leather strappy heels and a matching handbag.

Slipping gold hoops into my lobes, I eye the other pieces in the drawer and shove the most expensive looking ones into my purse. I don't even feel bad about it. I'll need to sell them for cash when I make my escape.

If Luca wants to use me and play me like a fool, then I'm going to take whatever the hell I want. He won't even know. He had Mrs. G do all the shopping.

After applying my makeup, I have just enough time to curl my hair before my hour time limit is up.

Looking in the bathroom's floor-length mirror, I take a deep breath, assessing myself.

I can do this.

I've worn an armor against the world for the past five years. I know how to show people only what I want them to see. Pulling my shoulders back, I raise my chin and walk out of the room and into the living room like I'm the one in control.

"I'm ready," I announce, and Leo and the other man look me up and down. "Problem?" I ask, turning my nose up like I believe I'm better than them.

"Not at all. Let's go."

I diligently follow behind the big scary guy, with Leo right behind me, and in the confines of the elevator, I can't hold my tongue any longer. "Is Luca too much of a coward to show his face now that the game has been played? I would've thought he'd want to see the look on my face when I found out."

"He'll be driving with us."

The elevator dings and opens at the garage level, and when I take a step off, I'm struck with the faintest hint of his scent.

He's here.

And when we walk around a large SUV, I spot him leaning against the door of a black Range Rover with his ankles and arms crossed, looking like he doesn't have a care in the world.

His face is devoid of all emotion, but his eyes still roam my body, his dark chocolate eyes turning molten. All he's seen me in are yoga pants and t-shirts because I refused to touch anything else in that closet, but now he can see what he's missing, the fucking bastard.

CHAPTER 18
Luca

She looks fucking beautiful.

She *is* fucking beautiful.

Makeup, no makeup. Hair done or up in a bun. Fancy clothes or stretchy pants and a loose tee. Or fucking nothing at all. I would have her naked 24/7 if I could.

But despite how amazing she looks right now, I see the pain she's trying to hide behind this false exterior. I left her in my bed this morning and it was the hardest thing I've had to do in a long time, knowing what was going to happen today, and knowing she was going to think the absolute worst of me.

Leo made me leave her there with him and Dante,

knowing I would want to tell her what was happening and try and get out of it.

This is important to him, I know. And I know he chooses Abrianna over anyone else any day of the week, but giving Angela back to those fuckers makes me sick.

"She's riding with me. Alone," I tell Leo.

"Dante's driving you," he says, and I nod, already knowing that. Leo walks over to his Range Rover where his body guard and driver, Alfie, is already waiting behind the wheel for him.

I open the back door for Angela, and she gets in without argument. She presses herself against the opposite door, trying to put as much space between us as possible.

Not happening.

I get in and slide over so I'm pressed close to her, giving her zero room to move.

"*Uccellino*, look at me."

"No. And I have nothing to say to you."

I turn her face towards me, but she keeps her eyes downcast. My anger flares. "Look at me," I growl, and her eyes dart up to mine. Those gorgeous honeycombs are crystalizing with her own anger.

Dante climbs in the driver's seat and starts the car, and Angela's eyes slide over to him. "Don't look at him. Look at me. He's not even here," I tell her, keeping our faces close so she has nowhere to focus but on me.

"I don't want to look at you. Let go of me."

"I know you're mad."

"Just shut up," she says fiercely. "You have no idea what

I'm feeling right now."

"Then tell me."

Her jaw clenches. "You had your brother and his henchman greet me this morning and tell me to get ready and look presentable because I was going back home. Today."

"You look beautiful," I tell her honestly, but I know it wasn't what she wanted to hear.

"You didn't tell me, Luca. And after yesterday…" She swallows, blinking rapidly and looking away.

"Tell me," I urge, pinching her chin so she'll give me her eyes again. I crave them like nothing else, and it hits me hard how much I've grown to need them.

Looking into them last night, I saw a future I never knew I wanted or could have. I don't know how I'm going to look into my own ever again if I hand her over today.

But that's the fucking job.

That's my burden to bear.

That's my duty to Leo as my brother and my boss.

"Yesterday, it was more. But now I know it's probably all been some kind of Stockholm Syndrome. You were my route to survival and I clung to that."

"You're lying, *uccellino*." I lean in a fraction more. "You and I both know you're too strong to fall to fucking Stockholm Syndrome. You feel it when I touch you," I say, sliding my hand across her cheek and down to cup the side of her neck. Her eyelashes flutter and her breath catches. "You feel it when I look at you. You feel it when I kiss you. You feel it when I'm deep inside of you, fucking you until you don't remember anything but my name that you scream out as you come so hard you pass out."

"Luca," she chokes out, her pulse racing under my palm "Stop."

"I can't."

Angela looks at me and I know she's about to say something, but the car stops and she shuts down again.

Pushing on my chest, she turns her head away.

I grip her chin again and force her back to me. "I'll find a way. But for now, you have to go back. Leo's woman's life is at stake."

"So is mine," she growls out. "But you don't have to worry about me. I've been looking out for myself long before you, and I'll be doing it long after you. I'll find my own way out and no one will ever find me or be able to use me in any of their sick games again."

Her words hit me like a fucking ton of bricks.

"Don't do anything stupid, Angela."

Scoffing, she slaps me across the face, and I'm too stunned to even react.

"No one's ever slapped me before," I tell her, more out of amazement than anger.

"That surprises me," she says sarcastically. "And don't tell me what to do. Besides, I'll be out of your hands soon. You should be happy to go back to whatever you did before you kidnapped me."

"I don't think I'll be able to," I admit, and again, I realize it's the wrong thing to say when I see the look on her face.

"I do. You got yourself into this situation, so don't pretend you care, and don't pretend you feel anything towards me."

Slamming my mouth down on hers, I shut her up.

I know this is all on me.

I know I have to give her back, but I want to keep her.

I want to be selfish for the first time in my life.

I want to let myself feel something other than my familial duty. I'm always following orders and doing what's expected of me. But for once, I want to disobey. I want to take something for myself. Which is probably why I took her in the first place.

Right away, I knew.

I saw her and knew.

This isn't a kiss goodbye, but a kiss to keep us both satisfied until I can get her back.

Because there's no fucking way this is the last time I get to taste her sweet lips, and last night sure as fuck wasn't the last time I found heaven in her sweet pussy that hugs me, strangles me, and makes me want to tie her to my bed so she's always there, ready and willing for me.

Sliding my tongue across her bottom lip, I pull away and lean my forehead against hers.

"I'm not pretending."

"It's too late, Luca. You made your choice, and now I'm making mine." She pushes me away. Fixing her hair, she gathers her purse in her lap. "Let's get this over with."

Dante gets out at her declaration and opens Angela's door for her. She flinches away from him. She never did that with me.

Taking a deep breath, I get my head on straight and step

out on my side, joining Dante and Angela on the sidewalk. She keeps at least a foot of distance between us as we walk into the deli, and I hate it. I want her close beside me. I want to show her brothers who's been taking care of her.

We closed Giorgio's for the day so we have the needed privacy, and at the long table we've had set up for us, Dante indicates where Angela will sit and then goes to stand at the end of the table with Alfie opposite him. Leo and I take our seats on either side of Angela and she visibly shrinks into herself, not wanting us so close to her.

We have men surrounding the building, and with us facing the windows that look out on the street, we have full advantage of the situation to see when Dom and Geno approach. If they're planning anything, we'll know, and we'll take them out long before they get close to us.

Right now, I need to be Luca fucking Carfano.

I need to be the underboss of the most powerful family on the east coast.

I can't let one pussy turn me into someone I don't recognize. Even if that pussy is a part of the most beautiful woman I've ever met and the fiercest little bird who isn't afraid of me or afraid to tell me what she thinks. It's a combination I've never had, and it turns me the fuck on.

Like right now. My cock is begging for the woman I'm about to hand over to be locked away again.

I have no right to want her, but as the silent minutes feel like hours passing, I count every breath she takes and can practically feel her heart beat through the strained air between us.

When two o'clock rolls around, a single black SUV pulls up outside, and the two pieces of shit climb out looking like smug bastards.

I want to punch that look right off their faces so fucking badly. They think they have the control here. They think they have the upper hand. They think they're winning.

But Carfanos always win.

I always win.

Giving them a false sense of control will let me do whatever I want since they'll think they're safe.

"Good afternoon, men," Dom greets with a smile as he walks through the door.

"Dom. Geno," is the only greeting Leo gives them.

They sit down in front of us, with their own two bodyguards standing beside them. Looking at me, and then Angela, their faces don't change into any look that could be construed as that of a concerned brother after their sister's been kidnapped.

"Angie, you look like they've treated you well," Geno says, his voice holding a tinge of disgust, as if he knows exactly what she's been doing all week.

Angela doesn't respond, though. She just tightens her grip on her purse in her lap and lifts her chin defiantly. My girl refuses to give in to her brother's shit, and I fucking love that.

"Did they take you to see our father? Or is he dead already?"

Out of the corner of my eye, I see her grip on her purse handles turn death-like, but she doesn't say anything. I can tell she hates this. She hates her family.

"Let's discuss the terms again. You get Angela and you keep your mouths shut to the Latin Kings. Because if you don't, believe me when I tell you, you won't know what's coming for you. I will rain hell down on your doorstep so fucking fast, you'll wish you never even came to me with the proposition to take your father in the first place."

"What?" Angela says softly, not caring that she interrupted Leo. "*You* had father taken?"

"Of course we did," Geno tells her. "How else could they have gotten in the house? But don't worry, dear sis, we'll make sure you're taken care of now."

Angela flinches, and I can't keep my mouth shut any longer.

"You'll show her the respect she's due," I tell them, and they both smirk.

"She got to you?" He sneers. "Has another one of the great Carfanos fallen to pussy?"

"She's your fucking sister," I grind out.

Dom smiles like a fucking psychopath. "She is. And she's coming home with us."

Angela's hands shake, and I can feel her fear and anxiety pouring off of her. I can't fucking stand it. Reaching under the table, I place my hand on her knee and squeeze gently.

She pushes it away. "Where's the bathroom?" Looking up at me, she tries to hide what she's feeling, but her defenses slip for me.

"Around the corner behind us," I tell her, and she stands, clutching her purse in front of her like a shield.

My girl is strong. She's—

Mine.

Angela is mine.

Fuck, that realization unlocks something inside of me that has me raging with the need to protect her from everyone, including her family. Especially her family.

I felt it when I saw her locked in her room on Long Island. I felt it when I woke to her screams. And I'm feeling it now, even stronger.

Angela is fucking *mine.*

I don't want her to ever be afraid again, and I want her to trust me with the secrets still haunting her. But first, I need to show her that I can be someone she can count on. She's not going with these fuckers. She's coming home with me.

"The deal's off," I announce, and Leo's head whips around to me.

"What the fuck are you doing?"

"Angela's not going anywhere with you," I tell Dom and Geno.

"Luca," Leo growls.

"Relax, Leo. They're not going to fight us on it."

"And why the fuck wouldn't we?" Geno asks angrily.

"You don't care about her."

"And you do?" He laughs. "She's useful to us."

"How?"

"Let's just say if we want to gain some of our father's business partners back, Angela will play a necessary role."

Blind rage flashes through me, and before I know it, I've leapt across the table and have Geno by the throat. Their guards aren't fast enough, and Dante and Alfie hold them back from stopping me while Dom just sits there watching, amused by my outburst.

"I'm going to fucking end you and your piece of shit family once and for all." Geno's face turns red from lack of oxygen, and I squeeze even harder, watching the light slowly drain from his eyes.

If killing him will keep Angela safe, then I'll bear that burden of another life taken on my soul.

"Luca, stop." I hear Leo's command from somewhere behind me, but I ignore him. His voice is far away as I focus on Geno and the feel of his windpipe in my grasp. "Luca. Now." His hand comes down hard on my shoulder, pulling me back. "Not here."

Angela's face flashes in my mind and I release her brother, stepping back and running my hands through my hair.

Leo grabs me by the collar. "What the fuck are you doing? Get your fucking head on straight."

"We're doing all of this for your girl, but *she's* mine. Angela is mine and she's not going with them."

Leo stares me down for a long few seconds before pulling his phone out. "Gabriel, send them in."

Five men flood in from the back of the restaurant and five through the front door.

"Take their men back to Long Island and dump them at the gates, and take Dom and Geno to the rooms right beside their father."

When it's just Leo and I left standing there, I feel the

weight of what he just did for me sink in. "Thank you." The words are unfamiliar to me, but they're the only ones able to express my gratitude.

"It all went to plan," he says, shocking me.

"What?"

"I just needed to get them to meet us. I wouldn't hand an innocent girl back over to those scumbags, and I knew they'd say something that would set you off. I thought it'd happen a little sooner, actually."

"You planned this? What the fuck, Leo?"

"You needed to fucking grow a pair and face losing her to see how much you need her." he shakes his head. "Jesus, I sound like a woman. Abri said it to me and it made sense, but I sound like a pussy. Just go fucking get her before I turn into one."

I can't help the small laugh that leaves me. Abri has him pussy-whipped, but he gets it, and I'll fight anyone who tries to take her from me.

I took her first. She's mine.

Heading down the hall where the bathrooms are, I knock on the door. "Angela?" I call out, "I'm coming in." When she doesn't protest, I push the door open.

She's not here.

The bathroom is small, with only two stalls and a vanity sink, so there's nowhere for her to hide.

What the fuck?

Storming out, I look back in the seating area and then push through the kitchen door.

Fuck. Fuck. FUCK!

Where the fuck did she go? We had this place surrounded!

FUCK!

We *did* have our men surrounding the building until Leo told them to get in here. Running to the kitchen exit door, the bright afternoon light hits me and I squint, looking both ways down the alley. I even check behind the dumpster in case she's hiding, but no, she's nowhere.

My chest constricts.

She left.

She left thinking I don't want her.

Slicing my hands through my hair, I grip the ends, growling in frustration.

"She's gone," I tell Leo, storming back inside.

"What do you mean she's gone?"

"She must've snuck out through the kitchen when the men came inside. I didn't think she'd bolt. She doesn't have a phone or money. Where is she going to go? What is she going to do?"

"Exactly. She couldn't have gotten far. Relax, Luca, we'll find her," he says with all the calm I don't currently possess. He pulls his phone out again. "Stefano, I need you to hack into all street cameras around Giorgio's and find where Angela went."

CHAPTER 19
Angela

Breathe, Angela. Breathe. I tell myself, trying to calm my racing heart.

I didn't know seeing my brothers again would be like that. They want me to be what my father did.

I can't.

Which means it's up to me to do something about it. No one is going to save me. I have to save myself.

Taking a few deep breaths, I look at myself in the mirror and square my shoulders.

"You've got this," I whisper.

Poking my head out the door, I hear a commotion and see a swarm of men come flooding from the kitchen doors I passed before, heading for the dining area.

It's now or never.

If I get caught, then what was going to happen, happens anyway. But if I can slip by unseen, then I can finally be free.

Walking on my toes so my heels don't make a sound, I sneak down the hall and duck right into the kitchen. Oh, thank God, there's no one in here.

Running towards the exit sign, I push the door open, finding myself in an alley. I could hide and wait it out until they leave, but I know Luca and my brothers. They'll scour this whole area for me. I have to go farther before laying low.

I run in the direction of the nearest street, checking left and right before choosing right, avoiding crossing in front of the deli. I walk as quickly as I can without drawing any attention, easily blending in with the other women on the street.

As long as I act like I'm okay, I will be. Once I start believing I'm not, and that I'm doomed to live a life that I have no control over, that's when I'm going to break down and find no reason to fight.

But I'm fighting now.

I'm not giving up hope until I've run out of every option.

I'm a stranger in this city with no phone, no ID, and no money other than the expensive jewelry I stashed in my purse this afternoon. I have no idea where I'm going, but I have no option other than walking.

I've lost count of how many blocks I've covered and how many times I've turned left or right to make my path a hard one to follow, but my feet are killing me and the sky has started to darken.

What am I supposed to do tonight? Where am I going to sleep?

My pulse picks up and my breathing shortens as panic sets in. I have no idea what the hell I'm doing. What was I thinking? I should've been looking for a pawn shop or something. Looking around me now, I see a pub up ahead, and I could cry from relief.

I can't even think straight anymore with how thirsty I am and how hard my feet are throbbing.

Pushing the door open, I see it's the perfect place to lay low for a little while. It's dimly lit, and has just enough people to hide amongst.

I can feel the eyes of everyone on me as I walk through the pub, but all I'm focused on is making it to the bathroom. I'm so exhausted.

After washing my hands, I fix my smudged eye makeup and dampen a paper towel, patting it around my neck to cool off before going back to the bar and sliding up on a stool.

"What can I get for you?" the bartender asks, his arms flexing beneath his t-shirt as he leans against the bar.

"Oh, just water, if that's okay?"

"Are you sure? You look like you could use something stronger."

He's not wrong. "I forgot my wallet before I went to a lunch meeting."

"Lunch?" He laughs. "It's dinnertime."

"Yeah…I've been walking a while."

His eyes widen. "Walking? Since lunch?"

I shrug, pushing my hair over my shoulder. "It wasn't a great lunch."

"Order whatever you want," he says. "It's on the house." His smile is charming, and I find myself smiling back freely. I don't know the last time I did that.

"Thank you. I'll have a water *and* a glass of cabernet, then." And since I already told him I don't have my wallet, there's no way for him to card me and see I'm only 19. I've been drinking wine every Sunday with our family dinners for a couple years now, so at least I know what to order.

"I'm Matt, by the way," he says as he pours.

"Angela."

"Beautiful name. It suits you."

"Thank you." Smiling, I feel my cheeks heat. He places my drinks in front of me and winks before walking over to someone flagging him down across the bar.

It suddenly hits me that I'm out in the city. Alone. I've spent my life behind the walls others forced around me, and now I'm free.

It doesn't feel like I thought it would, though. I thought I would feel lighter, but my chest is heavy with the weight of what I left behind. Or rather, who I left behind.

Luca managed to make me feel like I was someone worth something, and someone worth fighting for. I felt wanted and desired for the first time in my life.

But it was a lie.

My glass of wine quickly disappears as my mind swirls with too many emotions and thoughts that will only lead to heartbreak and tragedy.

I need to find a way to leave this city. I'll never be safe here or be able to live without looking over my shoulder. Whether it be my brothers or Luca and his brothers, someone will find me and force me back behind the walls.

Matt comes back around to me and pours me another glass without asking. "Thank you."

"Do you need to talk about it?" he asks sweetly.

"Not really." I shrug. "I wouldn't even know where to begin."

"Fair enough. But if you have a few more and feel like talking, I'm a good listener."

"I'll keep that in mind."

I sip my wine, looking around the bar at the other patrons. They're laughing, smiling, talking, and all seem to be carefree, enjoying life with friends and loved ones. I like that there's an eclectic feel to the types of people who are gathered here.

I've only gotten to see a bar on TV shows and in movies, so it's fascinating to actually be here. It's an atmosphere buzzing with life, and I wish I could be like them, just meeting up with friends for a drink after work, or meeting my boyfriend for dinner and a drink before we go dancing or to a movie.

Normalcy will never be my reality, though.

Even if I can make it out of the city, I don't think I'll ever be normal or whole.

Luca's rejection isn't something I'll be able to just get over in a few days. I gave more of myself to him than I have anyone else. Thankfully, not everything, though. I knew not to give him all of me.

I knew it wouldn't be a forever thing, Luca and I. But after last night…

After last night, I thought I saw something in his eyes that gave me hope that what we were doing wasn't just sex. But if I'm being honest, it never felt like it was ever going to be just sex for me.

I chose to let him inside of me.

Shooting back the rest of the wine in my glass, I huff out a deep breath and blink back the tears stinging at the backs of my eyes.

I can't cry. Not here. Not now. And certainly not in a bar full of people.

"Hey, you alright?" I look up at Matt and see concern written all over his face. He seems nice enough, and is good-looking too, but he's no Luca. No one is. No man could ever compete with him and his *presence*.

"Yes, thank you. I'm just realizing I'm running from something I don't want to run from. But I can't go back."

"Why not?"

"Because I'm not wanted there."

"That's hard for me to believe."

I give him a weak smile. "It's true."

"So where are you running to now?"

"I don't know actually. I don't even know where I'm going to sleep tonight. I'm trying not to dwell on that right now, though."

His brows draw together. "You don't have anywhere to

sleep tonight?"

"Nope." I take a sip of my water and run a hand through my hair. "You don't happen to have a spare booth in this bar I could use, do you?"

"No, but I have a spare couch at my place." Just as he finishes his offer, I feel the air around me shift, charged with an electric current that wasn't there before.

Matt's smile is wiped from his face and he takes a step back, the fear in his eyes telling me what I already know.

He's found me.

I turn my head to find Luca standing there, his dark eyes boring into mine. His face is made of stone, giving nothing away.

"Let's go," is all he says, and with two glasses of wine in me, my defenses are weak, and his deep voice resonates through me like an echo in a cave, bouncing all around.

"How did you find me?" I walked for hours, and it was all for nothing.

"You forgot who you're dealing with, *uccellino*. I have eyes everywhere."

"I'm not going back with my brothers."

"We're not discussing this here. Let's go."

"I'm not going with you either. Matt has generously offered to let me sleep on his couch."

The air around Luca swirls, his anger turning into a thick cloud of rage that has everyone in a close vicinity going quiet. Like when you don't want to spook a wild animal that looks ready to charge.

He looks past me to Matt, his eyes losing all sense of

humanity. "Is that right?"

His voice dropped to an octave that scares even me, and I don't want to be responsible for the death of a nice guy who offered to help me. I already know there's no helping me. And those who try, end up dead.

Turning back to Matt, I give him a small smile. "Thank you for the wine." His face has gone pale, managing to give me a small nod of acknowledgment that has Luca growling low under his breath.

I know he'll just drag me out of here if I don't go willingly, so I stand, but the wine I had has gone straight to my head on an empty stomach, and I grab the edge of the bar to steady myself, making Luca growl again.

He pulls out a wad of cash from inside his suit's jacket pocket and peels off a hundred, tossing it on the bar.

When the head rush subsides, I smooth my hands down the skirt of my dress and grab my purse. As I walk past him, Luca places his hand on my lower back and I don't flinch or try and escape his touch, instead welcoming it for the comfort it brings me.

And I hate that it does. It would be easier if my body didn't have a gravitational pull towards his, but it does, and I can't fight it.

Once again, I feel the eyes of everyone in the bar on me, except this time I know it's because I'm walking beside a man who screams wealth and power, demanding the attention of everyone in a one-hundred-foot radius. They can see I'm walking towards my death, and they watch with rapt fascination. The wild animal they held their breath for earlier is going in for the kill, and it's unavoidable and irreversible.

I'm trapped.

Outside, I find a waiting Range Rover with the big scary man with the scar waiting beside it, leaning against the passenger door, scanning the sidewalk for threats.

Luca opens the back door for me and I lift myself up inside, sliding to the far end. Unlike on the way to the meeting this afternoon, Luca doesn't slide right up against me. He stays to his side.

"I'm not going back to Long Island," I declare firmly, looking Luca dead in in the eyes. "I refuse."

"You're not going back with your brothers," he says, pulling his phone out.

"Then where am I going?"

"Back with me."

For now. I finish for him in my head.

It's a slow ride back to his building and we catch every red light there is, causing the air to get thicker and thicker with tension.

What he tried to tell me on the ride to the meeting repeats in my head. He said I feel it, and he's right, I do. But does he? Does he feel it when he kisses me? When he's deep inside of me? When he touches me?

Gripping my purse handles tightly, I keep my eyes on the window, watching the people we pass. It's like plane watching. I wonder where they're going and where they came from. Everyone seems to be on a mission as they walk. No one seems to just stroll leisurely. I used to walk the grounds of the compound, following the wall around the edges. I've always wondered what it would be like to walk through a meadow and know I could just keep walking without always having a wall just up ahead to stop me.

A lone tear rolls down my cheek and I quickly swipe it away discreetly, using the motion to run my hand through my hair, too. But when a few more escape, I can't swipe them away without drawing attention, so I let them fall, turning my face as far away as I can from Luca.

I learned how to hide my emotions a long time ago.

Pulling into the garage, it feels like a repeat of a week ago, and yet different, too. I know what's waiting for me upstairs and yet I still don't know what's going to happen next.

When the man with the scarred face parks the car, I use the sound of the doors opening and closing to take a deep breath and steady myself.

"Stay back, Dante," Luca orders.

Inside the elevator, I walk to the back corner, but Luca is done letting me hide.

I have my eyes cast down, watching his shoes walk right up to me while the doors close us inside.

"*Mia uccellino*," he purrs, running his fingers down my temple and jaw. "You weren't supposed to run."

My head snaps up. "I wasn't supposed to run?" I glare at him. "What was I *supposed* to do, Luca? Let you hand me over to my brothers so they could pass me along to whoever they wanted in their next business deal while I clung to the hope that you'd find a way?" I ask, my words dripping with sarcasm.

"Yes, that's exactly what you were supposed to do. Not go roaming around New York fucking City dressed like that with no money or phone or place to go. What the fuck were you thinking?"

"I was thinking that it was time I tried to take control of my life. But once again, I have none. Did you want to call my brothers tonight, or were you hoping to fuck me again beforehand?" My words spew fire, my fists clenched at my side. "And what's wrong with how I'm dressed?"

"You look too fucking good. Every man in that place had their eyes on you, and anyone could've taken you while you walked around for hours on end. Do you not care what happens to you?"

"No!" I yell in his face. "Not anymore!"

Luca's nostrils flare and his chest rises and falls with heaving breaths. When the elevator doors open, I slip around him, my heels clicking loudly with my pulse as I march towards his door. Luca is right there with me, and when he opens the door, I storm past him, heading straight for my room.

HA. *My room.*

It's not my room. This isn't my home.

"We're not done, Angela."

Turning on my heel, I face him, looking him straight in the eye. "We are." I slam the door and flick the lock into place.

Tears flow freely down my cheeks now that I'm alone, and I throw myself on the bed, not bothering to change my clothes. It doesn't take long before exhaustion takes over and

I slip into the bleak darkness that will probably be the rest of my life.

CHAPTER 20
Luca

She slammed the door in my face.

For the first time in my life, I don't know what to do.

I'm my father's son. He taught us that emotions cloud our judgement and only get in the way of what we have to do and be as Carfanos.

I know he never loved my mother. He said so on many occasions, justifying that he wouldn't have been able to build upon what his father started if he let emotions rule his decisions.

He was an asshole who beat his kids down to build them back up into the image he wanted. There wasn't a day that went by that Leo, Alec, or I didn't think about what it would be like to have anyone else as our father. But for all his faults, his fucked-up ways worked.

My brothers and I rule New York and New Jersey with iron fists. The other families, as well as the Triads, Bratva, Irish, and Armenians, have tried to take from us, but we always retaliate, and we always win.

Angela needs to realize that.

Pulling out my phone, I dial Leo as I pour myself a hefty glass of whiskey. "You have her?" he asks straight away.

"Yeah. Stefano tracked her to a bar in the East Village."

"Don't tell me she walked that far."

"Yes, she did," I growl, taking a gulp of my drink, the whiskey burning my throat before tamping down my anger. I still can't believe she was so reckless. "And yet *she's* pissed at *me*."

"Give her the night to cool down. It's not like she can leave."

"I know," I sigh, taking another long sip of my drink. "I need something to distract myself. Anything or anyone need rounding up?"

"Are you serious?"

"Yes. Give me a job." I haven't done street work in a while, but I can't be in the apartment, knowing she's here and I can't touch her.

"You want to do some Armenian recon?"

Knocking back the rest of my whiskey, I slam the tumbler down and head towards my office. "Yes. Where should I go?"

"Gabriel is leading a team at the edge of our Manhattan

blocks. I'll tell him to call you."

"Good." Hanging up, I grab two loaded magazines and slip them into my pockets. I already have my gun loaded in my shoulder holster from this afternoon, but I add an ankle holster and slide my smaller caliber gun into place.

I haven't done a recon mission in a while, but you always have to be ready. I went on one once with my uncle when I was first learning the business, and what was supposed to strictly be a surveillance mission, turned into a firefight that landed a few of his men with a few extra holes in them than they had before.

Sliding my switchblade into my pocket, my phone rings, and I look down to see it's Gabriel. "Hey, where am I meeting you?"

"You sure you want to come out tonight?"

"Yes," I clip, not wanting to explain myself.

"Meet me down in the garage. I haven't left yet."

"Be there in a few." I take one last look down the hall where Angela is, then shake my head and leave. I can't let her distract me.

"Hey," Gabriel greets, raising his chin.

"Let's go," is all I say, getting in his most discreet car – a black Audi A6. It will blend in and not set off any suspicions like a fleet of tinted black Range Rovers sitting all around the border of ours and the Armenian's territories.

"You want to tell me why you're out with me doing this?"

"No."

"I thought you found her."

"I did."

"Then why aren't you with her?"

"What the fuck is this? 20 questions?"

"If it'll get you to spill, then yes."

"She fucking hates me," I tell him, knowing this will be a long night if I don't give him something. "I betrayed her and her trust, and she hates me."

"Then what are you doing here with me? You should be convincing her otherwise. And if that doesn't work, maybe fucking her until she's not angry will make her understand."

"I'm going to pull out my gun and shoot you," I threaten, my vision blurring.

"You're willing to kill your cousin?"

"I didn't say I'd kill you. Just make you bleed so you'd shut up and mind your own business."

"But she is my business. She's every member of this family's business. She's a Cicariello. She's Joey's daughter, Luca. She has his blood running through her veins."

"She's not like him," I force through clenched teeth, trying not to lose my temper.

"How do you know?"

"I just do. And we're done talking about her."

Gabriel parks the car and shuts the engine off. "The Armenians used that alley three weeks ago as their dumping site." He nods his chin to the darkened alley across the street and up ahead, between a Chinese food restaurant and an apartment building. "They obviously wanted it to be found."

"They wanted to send us a message."

"Exactly. And we have teams stationed at their other

previous dumping sites we think they might use again."

"And why are you out doing it? Don't you have enough men to cover this?" Gabriel doesn't need to be doing the work himself either.

"Yeah, but Nick called me sick, and I was like you, wanting a little action to keep me busy. So, I took his post."

"Why, what's up?" Gabriel, Stefano, and Marco were raised alongside us when it came to training, but they had a better go of it with my uncle Tony as their dad. He was a bit more relaxed when it came to running his household since his sons weren't directly in line to take over.

"Nothing, man." He shrugs, not willing to share either. "I just needed to get out."

We sit in silence for a few minutes, and I can tell he wants to ask me something.

"Is she worth it?" he eventually asks.

I wait until my blood pressure lowers before answering with a curt, "Yes."

Gabriel takes my answer and doesn't pry further, and neither do I. I really don't want to talk about feelings and shit. I'm trying to get away from mine.

It's after midnight when the first drops of rain splash against the windshield, and after one when the headlights of a vehicle slowing down catches my attention.

"Hey," I say to Gabriel, pointing to the car. It slows further, and when it reaches the alley, it turns into it.

"It has to be them," he says.

"Let's go find out." Adrenaline spikes through me like it did when we were on the mission to take Joey.

"Wait." Gabriel's hand shoots out and grabs my arm. "I'm calling for backup." He quickly alerts the nearest team to meet us at our location.

"Let's go. I need a closer look to send Stef the license plate number."

"No. We're not getting into a shootout here. Too many potential witnesses and innocents."

I know he's right. If it is them and they see us, they won't hesitate to try and take us out.

"Fine. We'll follow them and have the men coming check the alley. If we can avoid the cops this time, it'll save us the hassle of making them look the other way. We can only avoid it so many times before someone higher up takes notice."

I try and catch a glimpse of who's in the car and what they're doing, but they're too far into the alley for me to get a good look at anything.

A minute later, they pull back out, and as they pass, I text Stefano their license plate number. Catching a glimpse of who's driving and in the passenger's seat, I quickly tell Gabriel, "It's them. Let's go."

Pulling away from the curb after another car passes, Gabriel keeps his distance as he follows them.

We go deeper into the Armenian's territory, and when the buildings start to become warehouses, my adrenaline spikes once more, ready for a little fun.

They pull into one of the buildings and we drive on, looping around and pulling into the lot of an abandoned building a block away. "Call for all teams to meet us here. I don't know how many they have."

"Already on it. And it's confirmed that they were dumping another body. Our guys took him and will take care of it."

"Good." I dial Leo.

"What the fuck, Luca?" he asks harshly. I look at the time and see it's after two, which means I probably interrupted something with Abrianna.

"We caught them dumping another body and it's being taken care of now. Gabriel and I followed their car back to a warehouse and we've called in backup."

"Are you fucking serious?"

"Yes."

"Don't be stupid. You're not going in there blind. We don't know what operation they're running out of there or how many men they have."

"Exactly. We're going to find out."

"Luca," Leo growls. "Cut the shit. We don't work that way. You're doing this because of Angela."

"Don't bring her into this. I've got this. You can stay in bed with your woman. I can't. I'll call when I know more." Hanging up on Leo, I turn to see Gabriel silently staring at me. "What?" I bark.

"Nothing. What's the plan?"

"We'll surround the building they went into to check for anyone on watch, and then we'll secure all exits and see if we can get a visual inside before breaching."

"Marco and Stef are coming in the van, and all the teams that were out are on their way, too."

Within a half hour, everyone is here, and we gear up as I explain to them the plan. "Alright, men. You all know your jobs. Let's put an end to this. Only shoot if you're shot at. If we can have a conversation and make a deal without making a mess, then that's preferable. But if not"–I shrug–"the world won't miss them." A few men laugh under their breath. "Dante will lead the way. Let's go."

With nothing to stay back and monitor, Stefano joins us, and he, Gabriel, Marco, and I follow behind a team of four men, with the other teams behind us to ensure our safety. Stef already checked, and they don't have any security cameras outside. They probably don't want to draw attention to the fact that there's an operation going on inside of there that requires security when all of the other buildings around it are run down and abandoned. It makes them an easy target.

We stay close to the walls of the buildings as we approach. Dante signals for the teams of four men each to peel off and surround the warehouse. I find a window that has a rip in the black fabric covering them and peer inside.

We're all linked with ear pierces, so I alert everyone else. "I can see five men sitting around a table playing cards. Another two sitting on their phones."

"There's only two entrances," Dante responds. "Team 3 stay on the front entrance in case they run. Teams 1, 2, and 4 will go in the back."

I'm on team two with Stefano, Marco, and Gabriel, and while we normally wouldn't all be present for this, I find myself amped up and ready for a fucking battle. I need this pent-up energy and anger to go somewhere.

175

I'm angry at myself.

For letting Angela slip away. For ever even considering sending her back. And for making her feel like she wasn't wanted. Because I fucking want her.

After Dante leads team one inside, with four following right behind, I take a deep breath and roll my shoulders back.

Shots are fired and voices start calling out to one another over our coms.

"There's more than we thought!"

"They're coming from everywhere!"

"Get down!"

"Fuck, let's go," I say, pulling my gun out and rushing through the door, right into the action.

It's all a blur as I run behind the nearest stacked pallet of what appears to be rice, and fire my gun off at every man I have in my sights. Peeking my head around the other side of the stack, I see one of them running for a back room.

"I'm going after one on the run," I say through my earpiece, not listening to the yelling in response telling me to stay where I am. I don't care that I'm not supposed to take unnecessary risks as the underboss. I can't sit back and let someone else tell me what to do.

I did that, and now I lost whatever trust I built with Angela.

The image of her beautiful face crumpled in disappointment and sadness when she found out I was in on sending her back to her brothers flashes in my mind.

I'm who my father wanted me to be – a man who puts the family first and doesn't care about anyone but himself.

I don't want to be that man anymore.

I want to be the man who found something and someone he doesn't want to lose, and hold onto her with everything I have. If I can't use my power and influence to save her and get what I want, then what the fuck is the point of any of it?

Running after him, I can feel the whiz of bullets flying by me, and I take their power, using them to make me feel invincible. Even when one hits my arm, it doesn't slow me down. It only angers me more.

I reach some kind of back office in the warehouse and find one of the heads of the Armenians gathering shit from a safe and shoving it in a bag.

"Diran." I smirk. "So good to see you again." Him and his brother run their operation together. Leo and I met with him after our father was killed to make sure the truce they had was still in place, and that our territory boundaries would remain. He knew not to fuck with us, just like he knew not to fuck with our father. And yet here we are. "It seems we have a few things to discuss."

"Luca," he grits out. "You come in here and open fire on me and my men. Why?"

"Why have you been leaving your competition for us to find? You try and bring attention to us, and we'll wipe you out." I shrug, showing him my indifference.

Diran smiles like the crazy bastard I know he is. "Took you long enough to find us. I just didn't think you were stupid enough to come here yourself. Now you get to die with the rest of your men."

"I think you have that reversed. It's you who will be dying with your men."

"We'll see."

I don't like the psychotic look in his eyes. My father warned us about him, saying he was the least stable man he's ever met. And that's saying something.

He clearly has an escape plan.

"I only wish you brought Leo with you, then I could've taken all of you out at once."

"RETREAT!" I yell through our coms so they all hear me over the battle going on out there. "GET THE FUCK OUT OF HERE!"

"What's going on?" Dante asks.

"Just get everyone out!"

"Will do," he clips, and I hear him shout orders to the men out on the warehouse floor.

"What did you do?" I ask Diran.

"I always have a failsafe escape plan for when shit doesn't go right," he says, pulling out a little remote from the safe behind him.

Shit, he's going to blow this place up?

"You're not doing jack shit until we're out of here. Let's go." Pointing my gun at him, he holds his hands up, but the detonator is in his left, and he gives me a slow smile.

I knew he was crazy, but the look in his eyes now is unlike anything I've ever seen. He looks like he's been sampling some of the product he pushes. Too much of it.

He looks ready to push that button. Like he can't wait to see what happens, not even realizing that he'd be dead if he did it.

His thumb starts moving up to the button and I have no desire to talk him out of it, so I go with the best option I have.

I shoot him right between the eyes. He doesn't deserve mercy.

I take the detonator from his open palm and look to see what he was packing from his safe. The duffel bag by his feet is filled with stacks of cash, so I grab it and then get out.

"Is everyone out?" I ask Dante.

"Yes. No casualties for us, and they're all dead."

"What happened in there?" Marco asks, running from around the building to me.

"Diran was about to blow us up is what fucking happened. I took care of him, but here"–I hand Dante the detonator–"now you get to blow him up."

Dante's lips lift slightly. I knew he'd want to do it. He has a penchant for destruction.

"Let's get out of here."

"What's in the bag?" Stefano asks as we walk back to the cars, and I hold it open for him to see. "Oh, shit. Okay."

"He was going to run, but when I caught him, he switched his play. Dante, how far of a range do you think that thing has?"

"We'll have to find out." There's a gleam in his eyes that reminds me I'm glad he's with, and not against, us.

My father brought him home one day when we were young and taught him to be the merciless killer, assassin, torturer, and everything in between that he is. Dante was an angry, quiet, broken street kid when my father found him, and he took the opportunity to give him a new life and purpose.

It's why he's known as the Executioner. If you see him, only death awaits you.

The teams load into their cars and quietly begin to drive off, leaving just Dante, Marco, Stefano, Gabriel, and myself.

"Let's light it up."

With a crooked grin, Dante presses the button and a light blinks red, and then green. The boom of the bomb shakes the ground where we stand a block away, and the night sky flashes yellow as the bomb blows the warehouse to smithereens, burning everything inside. Including any evidence that we were ever there.

"We have to get out of here before the cops come. This area is abandoned, but someone had to have heard that and will see the smoke."

On the ride back to our building in Manhattan, my adrenaline starts to fade, bringing with it the dull throbbing of my arm.

What the…?

Looking down, I see a hole in my jacket and blood soaking the surrounding fabric. Oh, right, I forgot about that.

"Shit, I was shot," I say nonchalantly, and Gabriel's head whips over to me.

"What? Where?"

"My arm. It's not bad. And keep your eyes on the fucking road," I berate, tugging the steering wheel so the car swerves back into our lane.

Pulling out my phone, I dial our on-call doctor and tell him to meet me in the medical suite.

By the time I get up there, I find both the doctor and Leo waiting for me.

"What the fuck, Luca?" Leo growls, his arms crossed and his face hard. "What made you think it would be alright for you to okay an impromptu raid that led to a shootout, you being shot, and then you blowing up a fucking building?"

"I did what was necessary. I made a decision."

"You don't get to make those when it involves our family and the best of our men."

I know I should've gone back to him with all the information gathered and waited until we made a plan like we did with capturing Joey, but I didn't want to wait.

"I know this is because of Angela, but you need to find another way to get your anger out. Hell, you could've just gone with Dante the next time he had a mark and killed the guy yourself. Jesus, Luca." Leo unlocks his crossed arms and rubs his forehead. "You could've been killed, not just shot. And Stefano, Gabriel, and Marco… I'm not losing anyone in our family because your head is messed up over a girl."

I reach him in three long strides, getting right up in his face. "Do you think I want that? Want this? But don't act like you're so fucking saintly. When it comes to Abrianna, you—"

"No," he barks, cutting me off. "I've never put the lives of our family at risk for her without a discussion and a plan. And when I couldn't have her, I sure as fuck didn't go and get myself shot because I was pissed off."

"The Armenians shouldn't be a problem anymore. Just

take this to the safe and I'll get sewn up." I shove the duffel bag at him and walk into the medical suite where the doctor has everything set up for me.

CHAPTER 21
Luca

Walking through the door of my place, lightning cracks across the sky, flashing the living room in its bright white light. Thunder rolls and I close my eyes, thinking of my nonna. She always said that thunder was the sound of angels bowling in heaven. She was a light in our family before she passed. My grandfather's heart. He only ever softened when she was in the room.

I know it's the same with Leo and Alec. The only time I see those fuckers soften is when their woman is in the room.

We made a pact when we were teenagers that we wouldn't let a woman destroy us. We could have as many as we wanted, but we knew letting one into our lives and hearts wouldn't end well.

It's just easier that way.

Another roll of thunder comes through with a flash of lightning lighting up the otherwise dark room, and I picture Angela lying in bed, the flashes of light dancing across her skin as I fuck her until she's screaming my name.

Shit.

The storm.

Running down the hall, I try her door handle, but she's locked me out.

FUCK! I didn't know it was supposed to storm again.

Tossing my ruined suit jacket down on my bed, I fish my spare keys from my bedside table and unlock her door.

She's not in the bed, and when I go to the bathroom, I find that door locked as well.

Cursing under my breath, the image of her crumpled against the toilet a few nights ago flashes in my brain.

"Angela," I call, but she doesn't answer. Pressing my ear to the wood, I hear her soft cries.

Unlocking the door, I open it and my chest twists at seeing her huddled in the shower, her knees tucked to her chest and her hands covering her ears with her eyes pinched closed.

She looks so small. So vulnerable. So fragile.

A broken little bird.

She's humming to herself, trying to drown out the sounds of the storm and send whatever memories have come to the surface, back to a place that's safe.

I crouch down so I'm at her eye level. "Angela," I say as

gently as I can. "*Uccellino*, look at me." Angela whimpers, but takes her hands from her ears to hug her legs

"Baby, look at me." Her face slowly lifts, her eyes connecting with mine, red from crying.

"You're here with me. You're not alone. I'm here. You're safe." I can tell my words are starting to sink in when her eyes come back into focus and lose their faraway look. "I'm here, Angela."

She gives me a barely discernable nod and I hold my hand out to her. It takes her a moment, but she reaches out and places her small hand in mine.

She really is fragile. I could break her so easily. But looking at her now, I see it's already been done in some capacity. Not fully, though. She's too strong to break.

Standing, I lift her into my arms and carry her to the sink so she can rinse her mouth out. Leaving her there, I go to the tub and run a hot bath, adding some of that powder shit to the water my sister insists I keep around for her if she stays here.

When I turn back to Angela, I find her haunted eyes on me, watching my every move. Without saying anything, I pick her up and stand her by the tub.

"I'm going to undress you, *uccellino*. Okay?" I don't want her to be scared of me. She already has enough demons living in her memories, she doesn't need to think of me as one, too.

Angela gives me another small nod and I undo the belt she has around her waist, then slowly slide the zipper of her dress down. She's still wearing the same clothes from this afternoon. Shoes and all.

I let the dress fall to the floor and it pools at her feet. Dropping to one knee before her, I unclasp the straps of her heels around her ankles and slide my hands around her calves. "Step out."

Removing her panties next, she steps out of those too, and I use every ounce of willpower I have to not let my eyes linger on her exposed flesh. It's a dangerous game I have no business playing right now.

Reaching around her, I unclasp her bra and slide it down her arms, letting it fall to the floor with everything else.

I want her to let it all fall to the floor. Everything she's holding inside. Everything that's keeping her from being completely here with me. Everything that has kept her from living the life of a fucking princess.

Lifting her in my arms, I gently lower her into the hot water. Thunder rolls again, and Angela shudders. I know I can help with that, too.

"Wait," she croaks, her voice laced with panic. I stop mid-step. "Don't go."

My heart twists at the sound of her pain, and when I turn back, I see it etched all over her face.

"I'll be right back. I wasn't going to leave you." Just outside of the bathroom, there's a panel on the wall that controls the temperature of the room and the surround sound system. I turn on the bathroom speakers that are hidden in the corners, and choose a playlist that's all instrumentals, turning the volume up to drown out the thunder.

Stepping back into the bathroom, I see Angela's face

relax just the slightest at my return.

I know she's experienced her own agony today, but so have I. And I know I shouldn't, but I start to undress. I need to hold her. I need to know she's here with me just as much as I want her to know I'm not fucking going anywhere.

She doesn't protest, in fact she slides forward so I can climb in behind her.

Not caring that I have fresh stiches in my arm, I pull her back against me and she places her hands over mine on her stomach.

"Close your eyes, *mia uccellino*. Just listen to the music and breathe."

Angela's chest rises with a deep breath in, and falls on her exhale. After a few more, her body begins to relax against mine.

The jets of the jacuzzi tub hit us from all directions, aiding in calming her. The only time I've been relaxed as of late has been when I've gotten to hold Angela in bed.

It's my fault she's like this. I shouldn't have left her alone tonight.

Reaching for the soap and luffa on the built-in shelf within the tiled wall, I begin to wash her gently and Angela continues to breathe deeply, allowing me to give her this comfort. The fact that she's letting me, fills me with a strength and power different from what I feel and use as Leo's underboss.

Angela hates me for what I did. I hurt her just like her father and brothers, and yet she's letting me see her like this. She's letting me touch and heal her, bringing her back to me.

She's mine, and I'll do what I have to so she knows that.

CHAPTER 22
Angela

Being in Luca's arms again makes me feel safe and cared for.

I hate him, and yet I need him.

He's the only one who's ever made me feel safe. He has the power to take me away from it all and bring me back to the present when my mind is stuck in the memories of my past.

Luca gently cleans me, lulling me into a haze of comfort and safety I could never achieve on my own. I wish I could always feel this way.

I don't know how long we lay in the tub, but Luca eventually turns the jets off and drains the water, standing with me in his arms. He pats us both dry with a soft towel I barely feel against my skin and carries me out of my room and over to his, setting me on the edge of his bed.

He disappears into the closet and comes out in a pair of sweatpants, holding a t-shirt. He lifts my arms up and slips the tee over my head, making sure to pull my wet hair free from the collar. His shirt is soft against my sensitive skin, and with every breath, his scent fills my lungs, allowing my fractured mind to weave itself back together.

My eyes roam over him, landing on a bandage covering his upper left arm. "What happened?" I ask, still in a daze.

"I was shot."

My brows come together, confused. "Shot? When?"

"I needed to clear my head. To keep myself occupied."

"So you went and got yourself shot?"

"I'm fine. It's just a flesh wound."

He brought me back up here and then went out and did something to distract himself that got him shot? I can't even deal with, or process that, right now.

Laying down, I breathe in more of his scent that's everywhere as Luca turns the lights out and closes the curtains so I can't see the lightning that's still flashing outside.

"Come here, *mia uccellino*," he whispers, sliding in behind me. His large body molds to mine for only a moment before he's flipping me so I'm facing him. "I need to see your eyes, baby."

My hearts flutter in my chest and I blink, focusing my eyes on his. They churn my insides.

"I didn't know it was going to storm," he says softly,

running his fingers through my hair.

"You weren't here," I croak, not able to hide how weak I feel. I don't like to admit that I need help, but I know I would've been okay if he was here, and he wasn't.

"I'm sorry," he murmurs, and I feel his apology bone deep, the two words resonating within me as the gifts I know them to be. Men like him don't say they're sorry. They take what they want, do what they want, and say what they want without remorse.

"Tell me, *uccellino*," he urges. "Let me take the pain for you. You shouldn't carry it alone any longer."

"I don't think I can," I whisper, my throat tight. I don't think the words will form. They've been buried for so long.

Luca brushes his thumb across my bottom lip. "I know you can."

Swallowing hard, I slide my hands to his chest, feeling his heart beat beneath my palm – strong and steady.

He believes in me.

He wants to know everything, and I want to tell him, but I don't know how. Closing my eyes, I inhale Luca's exhale, his air filling me with the strength I need to put a voice to the memories and monsters that have been haunting me.

"I was always sheltered and kept hidden away, but after my mom died…" I begin, blinking away tears. "She was the only good thing in my life. The only person I've ever trusted. But when she was gone…that's when everything went from bad to worse."

"I…" I hesitate, that one syllable holding the weight of my next words. "I was fourteen, and we were still living in the city. My father sent me to my room, but I expected it because he always did whenever he was having a business meeting. It gave me a chance to be alone and miss my mom without being yelled at for mentioning her." I blink, and a lone tear falls. "I fell asleep reading, and then–"

No.

Looking into Luca's eyes, I plead with him to know without me having to say it. But I know I need to. He needs me to.

"He barged into my room. A man I've never seen." My voice shakes, and Luca strokes his thumb across my cheek, reminding me he's here. "At first, I thought something had happened and he was coming to rescue me or tell me I had to leave, but he closed and locked the door behind him. That's when I knew it wasn't right."

I can't stand the intensity of Luca's eyes, so I find a spot over his shoulder as I dive into the memory that's been the noose around my neck, slowly tightening and cutting off my air supply for years, just waiting to fully claim me as its victim. I'm not a victim anymore, though. And the only way to break free from the stranglehold is to purge.

"I held the blanket as tight as I could, like it was a shield. But he ripped it away. I screamed, but no one came. No one helped me. Not my brothers down the hall, and certainly not my father."

Sucking in a shaky breath, my eyes flit to his and then back to the safe space of nothing above his shoulder. "I fought. I fought him as hard as I could, but I was weak and small. He told me to shut up and take it like a good little girl.

He said that my father told him I would be good for him."

I can feel his rough grip on my arms again, so I press my fingers deeper into Luca's chest, the hard beat of his heart keeping me rooted to the present even when my mind has gone back.

Tears streak my cheeks and spill onto Luca's hands as he strokes my face.

"I didn't leave my room for days. Maids brought me food and water, but no one else came. They all knew. They heard. My father came to me five days later. He told me it was necessary for the family, and now that my mother was gone, it was my job to cater to his business partners. My brothers didn't look me in the eye for a while, but eventually they did. They, too, accepted my new role in the family."

Pausing, I take a breath.

"It wasn't just that one time," I confess softly, my mouth coated in acid. With the beat of Luca's heart strong under my touch, I do as he wanted and give him everything I'm feeling. He's strong enough to hold onto it for me. He'll know what to do with it and know how to handle it better than I ever could.

"There were three of them, but that first man…" I pause, and Luca pinches my chin.

"Stay with me, Angela. Look at me." I take a deep breath and look into his dark chocolate eyes.

I let him in.

I know he can see everything when his eyes drop their walls too. I can feel him inside of me, swimming through my soul.

He gives me the strength to continue.

"The first one… He was worse than the others. He was pure evil. It seeped from his pores, fell from his tongue, was in every look, and felt in every touch. He's who I have nightmares about. The other two were gentle compared to him, and they weren't gentle."

Luca is trembling with rage, his hand on my face shaking as he tries to contain it, but I can see it written all over his.

I reach up and cup his cheek. "Luca?"

"I'm good, baby."

"You don't look okay."

"Don't worry about me. I want you to keep going. Tell me everything."

I slide my hand back down to his chest before continuing. "I see him in my nightmares. He's waiting for me with that look on his face that means he can't wait to hear me scream. He got off on hurting me any way he could. I quickly realized that fighting him only made him more violent and made him want more, so I tried not to speak. I tried not to fight. I tried not to scream when he…" I look away. "But I couldn't help it. It's not in me to be quiet and docile. It's not in me to just lay there and take it like a good girl." My throat is raw and cracks at the end of my confession.

"Whenever there's a storm, the sound of thunder brings me right back there to the last time, before we moved to our Long Island home full-time. Flashes of lightning gave me glimpses of his face while he was on top of me, and the thunder rolled when he hit me.

"It took me years to be able to reach a point where I

didn't see him or the others every time I closed my eyes. But when it storms, I can't help it. I'm right back there. Right back in that room. Right back to being 14 and weak."

"You're not weak, Angela," he says fiercely, with conviction.

"I hated being locked away in that house, but it was safe there. My father didn't have his business partners over anymore once we moved."

"That's because my family took all of his businesses, *uccellino*. We took everything from him, piece by piece. Which is why he moved you to Long Island. To hide like a coward instead of facing what was coming for him." His eyes bore into mine. "My family and I. We were coming for him. We *did* come for him."

"That's when you found me."

"Yeah, baby." He slides his fingers through my hair and pulls me closer. "And you're never going back," he assures me, fisting my hair and tugging gently.

A new wave of pain hits me. "You were sending me back."

"When the boss gives an order, I listen."

"He says jump and you say how high?"

"Something like that," Luca murmurs, and I try and pull away, but his arms are like an iron cage keeping me exactly where I am. "I couldn't go through with it. Leo knew I was never going to before I even did. When I saw your brothers and heard how they spoke to you...I knew they were a part of what you couldn't tell me. I knew they weren't there as your brothers to make sure you made it home safely. I felt your discomfort and your fear, but you ran before I could tell you that you were coming back with me."

"That doesn't change the fact that you were going to hand me over like a piece of property. If they kept their mouths shut and were better at hiding their intentions, you would've sent me back. My father owned me, so you took me. And now that you have him, the ownership is passed to my brothers, and they think they have the right to have me back so they can use me like my father did."

"That's never happening," he growls, his hand tightening in my hair. "You're mine."

"I'm not," I whisper.

"Yes, you are. I did go there with the intention to hand you over, but when I was faced with losing you"–he shakes his head slightly–"it made me see how much I fucking need you. You're mine, *uccellino*. I have your father and I have your brothers. They can't hurt or use you anymore."

"I'm not yours, Luca," I whisper. "I could never be yours."

"Why not?"

"Because I'm broken. Those men took a piece of me that I can't have back. But when I was with you, I didn't feel so broken. That's why I didn't want to tell you. I didn't want you to see me as damaged or dirty or a broken bird you didn't want to touch anymore."

My heart twists in my chest and I pinch my eyes closed, the pain lacing through me at saying aloud what I never had the courage to even think, is too much.

"Angela," he admonishes, but I can't take my words

back. The only reason I told him was because he's lulled me into a false sense of security.

He makes me feel like I'm safe, but I'm not. As long as I'm around him, I'll always be at risk for a repeat of my past. I'll always be vulnerable.

"*Mia uccellino.*" My heart twists at his name for me. It feels like the beautiful summer afternoon sun against my skin, warming me and giving life to my soul. "I don't see you that way. And what happened to you, what you went through, it doesn't make me want you any less. In fact, I want you more. I want to replace every bad touch and experience with my own. I want you to trust me with your demons and let me fight them with you."

"Luca," I whisper, my mind spinning.

"I want to give you everything. I want you to have everything."

"You can't give me what I need, Luca."

"The fucking hell I can't. I can give you the world, Angela. Name it and it's yours."

"I don't need *things*. I never did. All I've ever wanted is to be free."

"You're free from your father and your brothers. I have them."

"That's not what I meant and you know it. I can't do this anymore. I can't be held captive and shuffled around like a chess piece, just waiting to be sacrificed."

"I'm not sacrificing you. You're the fucking queen. You're protected."

"The queen isn't protected in chess. The king is. The

queen fights, protecting herself. Which is what I want to do."

"Angela," he pleads, sounding pained.

"You should want me gone. I'm nothing but the daughter of your enemy that you took because you liked the way I looked. You liked the idea of having me and having something to lord over my father. But he doesn't give a shit, and neither do you. I don't trust you, Luca. Not after today."

His eyes harden at my declaration and he throws his defenses back up.

"You got what you wanted all along, though," I continue. "You got me to reveal why I hate my father and why I want him to be punished. But I'm not a little bird you can keep locked away. If you do, I'll always want to fly free. I'll always wonder what it's like out there. No matter how pretty the cage I'm put in, and no matter how my captor makes me feel."

I looked up what *uccellino* means when I got my laptop, and while I thought it was sweet, I now see it differently.

His eyes turn to hardened coal, ready to be lit on fire. I can feel him thrumming with an electric current that could power the storm outside.

"Captor." He spits the word out like it's a curse. Like it's dirty. "You still think I'm your captor?"

"What else would you be? You took me and have kept me locked in here."

He skims his fingers down the side of my neck and circles them around my throat lightly. "You haven't seen me be your captor, baby." His low voice sends a chill down my spine and I see the true nature of him lurking on the outskirts of his eyes.

He has the capacity to be someone's worst nightmare. Worse than my father or brothers could ever be. But he wouldn't be mine.

Regardless of whether or not I trust him, I know he wouldn't harm me physically.

That doesn't change anything, though. I still can't stay.

"I can't be a prisoner my entire life. I need to see what's out there for me. You may say I'm yours and that you weren't going to give me back, that you couldn't, but that doesn't change what I need."

Luca drops his hands and slides away from me. I feel the loss immediately and yearn for his warmth, but I know this is it. This is all we are and all we can be.

Slipping out of his bed, I feel Luca's eyes on me as I walk to the door. With my hand on the handle and my back to him, he doesn't say anything and he doesn't try and stop me. I know what I said, but I still held onto a small hope that he would try and make me stay and change my mind.

It's stupid, though. Luca isn't the type of man to make declarations of love. Mafia men don't know real love. They only know the power, dominance, and manipulation that's ingrained in them to get and stay ahead of everyone else. It's stupid of me to think I could be the exception to that.

Squaring my shoulders, I put my invisible armor back on. I gave him something I can't get back. I gave him my past. But that doesn't mean he gets my future, too. The future is mine to choose. Even if Luca keeps me here, I can't let him in again. *I'm* deciding that.

Stopping myself from sliding anymore down the rabbit hole of Luca, I have to climb back out. Falling for him isn't something I can do. I would give him everything I have inside of me. Even more than he's already claimed. He'd know every dark corner of me – every secret, every thought, and every feeling.

I can't do that.

I can't be that girl.

I could only be her if he could give me what I need.

Closing the door behind me, I go into my room and crawl right into bed, hugging the comforter around me as tightly as I can, needing the security it provides. My shield to everything, it keeps my breaking heart from escaping, and keeps whatever is out there from getting to me.

I just want to be alone.

CHAPTER 23

Luca

My blood fucking rages through me. Joey is going to die a slow and painful death. Angela's brothers are going to die a slow and painful death. Those fuckers who laid their hands on her are going to die slow and painful deaths.

Anyone who's ever hurt her is going to die.

Angela wants freedom. She wants what I can't give her. I can't give her a life of freedom and roaming around without a care in the world.

What I can give her is vengeance. It's what I know. It's what I was raised to do and embody. While she battles her demons on the inside, I'll make sure her demons are slayed out in the world.

I was done the moment those honey eyes met mine. I knew she was going to wreck me, and yet I willingly let her. I let her crawl under my skin and into my heart, and now it beats for her. Every breath is for her.

Climbing out of bed, I throw on a t-shirt and head straight for my office to call Leo. "I need to talk to you. It's important."

"Basement in ten," he says curtly, knowing I wouldn't bother him in the middle of the night again if it weren't important. Especially after what happened.

Angela closing the door on me was final for her. And God fucking knows she deserves a better man, but there isn't one who would do what I'm going to for her.

When the doors open to the basement, there's no one down here except Dante who's using the punching bag like it's actually fighting back.

Leo's already waiting for me in the conference room, and I take a seat across from him, running my hands down my face.

"What's going on, Luca?"

"She told me everything, Leo."

"What's everything?"

"She's not good with storms, and I came back before to find her in bad shape. Joey, Dom, and Geno need to pay." I slam my fist down on the table. "I'm going to make them suffer and feel the pain they caused her. They fucking used her, man." The look in her eyes as she replayed her memories flashes before me. "They used her in the worst imaginable, and despite her trusting me with her past, she's done with me. I can't give her the freedom she wants. And I get why she wants it. She's been hidden away her entire life and wants out."

"And all you want to do is hide her away to keep her safe," Leo finishes for me.

"Yes."

"What do you want to do?" he asks carefully.

"You know what it's like to put Abrianna first, what do you think I should do?" I've never come to Leo for help like this before, but I don't want to fuck it all up.

"Abri didn't want me to leave, though."

I narrow my eyes. "Thanks for pointing that out."

"You really want me to tell you what I think?"

"Yes," I hiss.

"Let her go." I open my mouth to say something, but he holds his hand up. "Just listen. She has to see for herself what's out there. The world she thinks she wants will let her down. I saw the look on her face when I told her she was going back home, and it was a look of someone who didn't want to leave here. Leave you."

"I betrayed her."

"You were following my order."

"She's been put second her entire life and treated like a pawn, moved wherever she was needed. I did the same thing."

Leo stares at me, studying me. "Put a guy on her to make sure she's safe, but let her go."

I know he's right.

I can't force her to stay with me.

She's still so young. She deserves a chance.

"I can't yet. I need to talk to Joey."

Leo nods. "Let me know if you need anything."

"I will." Standing, I stretch my neck out and head to the hall of cells. Each step has me shedding every thought and feeling I have other than my anger and need for blood.

Joey is laying on the floor sleeping, huddled and shaking under a thin blanket. He pops up the moment the heavy metal door opens.

"Get the fuck up." Grabbing him by the shirt, I haul him over to the metal chair bolted to the floor and secure his ankles and wrists to it with the cuffs attached.

"I know you plan on killing me. Why don't you just do it?" he goads.

"Because death is too easy for you, Joey. It'll come eventually, but not yet. First, I need some information."

He laughs. "Of course you do."

"Shut the fuck up," I growl, gripping his throat. "You have nothing left for yourself. We've taken your livelihood. We've taken you. We've taken your sons. And we've taken your daughter. There's no one left, and there's nothing left for you."

"Then why would I tell you anything?" he manages to choke out.

"Because I know what you did to Angela, and I decide how and when you die. See where I'm going with this?"

The whites of his eyes turn red from lack of oxygen. I loosen my grip. "What lies did that little bitch tell you?"

Tightening my hand again, I feel his life at my mercy. His

pulse is pounding and his mouth is opening and closing with nothing coming out.

"Call her that again and I'll bring someone in here that will show you the meaning of being a little bitch. He'll do to you what you had done to your daughter, you filthy piece of shit. He'll own your ass. He'll fuck you until you bleed. And even then, he'll come back for more."

The fear in his eyes reminds me of Angela.

"Does that not sound like fun? You had no problem giving your daughter to your filthy business partners to use as they wanted."

His eyes start to glaze over and I release him in a flash. He doesn't get to die yet.

Joey sucks in ragged breaths, the blood draining from his head as the oxygen returns to his lungs. "She knew her place."

His cheek bone cracks beneath my fist. "That wasn't her place. She deserved to feel safe in her own home. She deserved a family who cared about her."

"She deserved whatever I let her have."

I can't stand the sound of his bullshit anymore. "Tell me their names."

"What's it worth to you?"

Everything.

I punch him again. "I'll put a bullet between your eyes."

"Not good enough."

"What's not good enough is you," I spew angrily. "You weren't a good enough father or husband. Now, you're going to tell me their names or I'm going to make good on my earlier threat. Then I'm going to use every method of torture my father taught me. Your screams will make me sleep better."

I see the blood drain from his face as he sees the truth in mine. I don't make idle threats. As a man in my position, I know how to find the right person for every job. It wouldn't take much for me to reach out and find a sick fuck who enjoys putting another man in his place and revels in his pain.

"Names. Now," I snarl, but Joey keeps his lips pressed together. "Don't fucking test me. You'll regret it." He just stares me down, as if he has the power to intimidate me right now. "No? Alright, I'll be right back."

Leaving him alone in the room, I go to the artillery we have on the other side of the conference room and shooting range. It's loaded with every type of weapon you could think of, but I go for a Glock 19. I also pocket a switch blade and brass knuckles. I haven't gotten to use those in a while.

Joey looks up at me wearily when I reenter, and I give him a wide grin as I hold up my gun, fully knowing I resemble a psychopath, which makes him flinch.

"You've been locked in here for over a week. I don't know what gave you the impression that you have a choice in whether or not you talk."

I press the barrel of the gun to his forehead and the one side of his mouth twitches up in a half smile of sorts.

We can play if he wants.

Dropping my arm, I pull the trigger, and his smile is wiped from his face, replaced with agony. I shot him in the foot, but he doesn't scream, just grunts while his face turns beet red from holding it in.

Let's try again.

I lift my arm again and pull the trigger, the bullet ripping through his left shoulder this time.

"FUCK!" he yells, and I smile.

"Good. You're talking."

"Fuck you, Carfano!" he grits through clenched teeth.

"You'll be the one getting fucked unless you tell me the names." I step on the top of the foot I shot and press the barrel of my gun into the wound on his shoulder, finally making him scream.

"Okay! Okay!" He pants, his face draining of color. "Albert Ferarro." I press my foot down harder on his. "James Vick." I press the gun harder into his shoulder. "AHHH!" He screams. "Chris Travino!"

"Which one was it?"

"Was what?"

Pistol whipping the side of his head, I press it back into his shoulder. "Don't play stupid. The one who fucked her up the worst. The one who no doubt told you beforehand that he was a fucking sadist and couldn't wait to ruin her."

All I see is red.

All I hear is my blood pounding in my ears.

All I feel is hatred.

All I want is to see this worthless piece of shit in front of me pay for the sins he had done to his daughter.

I lower my gun to his other foot and his eyes go wild. "No! It was James!"

"How do I know if you're telling me the truth?"

"Because he demanded a virgin for our deal to go through. He wanted someone he could break in "

My hand shakes with the need to pull the trigger and end his life. But I can't. Not yet.

"You better not be lying, or I'll come back and make sure you have enough holes in you to sink to the bottom of the fucking Hudson."

Leaving him, I stalk down the hall and go back to the artillery, tossing the bloodied gun, brass knuckles, and knife down on the nearest counter before heading back to the elevators. Dante is still going at it with the bag, his eyes only sliding towards me for a second before his focus is back on his combinations.

When the doors slide open on my floor, I stare at the front door, but don't make a move towards it.

I can't go in there.

If I go in, then I'll want to go to her. I'll use every tactic I have to show her how good staying would be.

And I can't do that to her.

Not after what she told me.

Pressing a button, the doors close again, and I head down a few levels to an apartment I know is empty. We always have a few unoccupied for guests and out-of-town family. My access code and retinal scan is a skeleton key for the entire building, and once inside, I go straight through to take a shower.

Under the hot spray of water, I scrub my hands over my face.

I want her in here with me. I want to feel her soft skin

under my touch as I rub her body with soap. I want to hook one of her legs over my shoulder and devour her sweet pussy.

I want what I can't have, and now my cock is as hard as steel, needing his new home. But I can't have her, so my hand will have to do.

Closing my eyes, Angela's face comes front and center with her honey eyes looking at me with absolute trust, and it doesn't take long before I'm shooting my load on the wall. Leaning my forehead against the tile, I let the water beat down on me until my exhaustion kicks in.

I'll call a meeting tomorrow to fill everyone in, but I haven't slept well in a few nights, and I collapse into bed.

CHAPTER 24
Luca

Sitting around the conference table, the eyes of my family are on me.

"I'm letting Angela go," I announce.

"Why?" Nico asks.

"Because she wants to go."

There's a stunned silence. "That's it?"

"That's all you're getting. Her past and my reasons are mine to know, no one else's." I look each of them in the eye and they give me small, discernable nods in response. "But before I let her go, I need to do something for her."

"If she's yours, Luca, we're doing this together," Leo says. "Unlike your little showdown with Joey last night."

"What did he do with Joey?" Marco asks.

"I just shot him a couple of times." I shrug. "He had information I needed and he needed some motivation in order to hand it over."

"What information?"

"Three names. We need to find them."

"And then what?"

"And then I'm going to kill them."

"Alright, what're the names?" Stefano asks, his fingers already flying across his keyboard.

"Albert Ferarro, Chris Travino, and James Vick."

"When we took over Cicariello's businesses, we made sure to keep track of who we gave what to. So, if they're his associates, let me pull up the most recent reports." Stef's brows crease for a minute and then smooth out. "Got them. Forwarding their addresses to you now."

"We'll go tonight," Leo decrees. "Gabriel, Marco, and Stefano, get your men ready. You'll each take one of the names and bring them here."

* * * *

Waiting with Leo in the basement for the men to be delivered, I can't sit still.

"Jesus fucking Christ, Luca. Sit down and wait."

"I can't."

"They'll be here soon. There's no way they would know we're coming or have time to escape."

"I know. I just…" I run my hands through my hair,

pulling on the ends. "I need to do this for her."

"And once you do, then she's gone."

"Yes. She's given me a new purpose."

"She'll still be your purpose even when she's not here, Luca. Just grow a fucking pair and do what needs doing. Be her man. Be her savior. Be whatever the fuck she needs. Now, go to the shooting range. You need to relax."

"They'll be my shooting range."

Leo huffs out a breath. "Whatever you want. But all your pacing is annoying the hell out of me."

Our phones beep with a message. *They're here. Coming down now.*

"Leo, I'm letting you know now that Dom and Geno need to be put down, too. They all do. They were all in on it. No one helped her. No one cared."

"You care. That's all she needs. Just one person to care about her more than anyone else. We grew up with the same father who was determined to turn us into heartless bastards. He almost succeeded."

"Almost."

"Exactly. Remember that. And use your anger to do this for her."

I already planned on doing that.

I wait in the gym area, pacing until Gabriel, Marco, and Stefano march the three men towards their certain deaths. Towards me.

I know who is who from their pictures, and while I thought I wanted them to have slow and painful deaths, seeing them now has me realizing they don't deserve to breathe another second longer on this planet.

"What the fuck is going on? Why are we here?" Albert asks, his eyes moving wildly around him. In his fifties now, he's the oldest of them, and just the thought of him touching my precious Angela when she was only 14 has my fingers itching to kill him first.

"No one said you could speak," Gabriel chastises, pushing him forward.

Chris is next to come in, and I can tell he already knows why he's here.

James Vick.

He's last to walk into the gym and onto the grappling mats, his smug, arrogant face smirking at me as he passes by.

Wiping that look from his face will be the most satisfying of them all.

"Have you figured out why you're here yet?" I ask, stepping towards them.

"Why don't you tell us," James says sarcastically, feigning disinterest. But I see the uncertainty lurking behind his douchebag exterior.

"Angela Cicariello." Her name incites a flash of knowing across each of their faces, and I give them a cruel smile. "I see you know exactly why you're here now."

"What the fuck do you care about some young pussy we fucked years ago?"

My eyes go blurry with rage, and without thought, I pull my gun from behind my back and aim it at James. "If you say one more thing about her like that, I'll drag your death out until you're so unrecognizable, I won't even know who I'm killing at that point." My voice drops to an octave that vibrates through the air like a swarm of bees

I didn't want my family knowing Angela's secrets, but this fucking asshole just spelled it out for them. I can feel them behind me, their own anger at knowing what this is all about rippling out from them, sending the room's tension up tenfold.

He smiles right back. "Did you fall in love, Luca? I doubt she's as good as she was when I had her. She wasn't broken in yet."

A growl akin to a wild bear comes out of me and I pull the trigger, making sure I only hit his arm. Rushing him, I grip him around the throat and throw him to the floor. His face turns red and the smug look finally disappears.

"I'm going to save you for last, Vick."

Releasing him, I stand and press the barrel of the gun to Chris's head. "You touched her. Now you die."

The bang of the gun and thud of his body hitting the floor loosens one of the weights that's trying to cave my chest in.

Going down the line to Albert, I press the barrel to his head next. "You touched her. Now you die." I repeat the mantra, and another weight loosens on my chest at the bang of the gun and his body hitting the floor.

"Now, James," I start, wiping Albert's blood from my face. "I know what you did to her."

"Does the little cunt still have nightmares?" he taunts, pulling himself up to stand again. "Does she close her eyes and see me, then scream? I always loved it when she screamed."

"SHUT THE FUCK UP!" I blow up, not able to hold it in any longer. Gripping his throat, I toss my gun aside and shove my hand in my pocket, slipping on the brass knuckles.

I hit him.

I hit him over and over again.

Blood splatters up at me and spills from his face as the metal rips his skin open, exposing him for who he is – a monster.

No one dares to stop me. They heard him.

"You don't get to haunt her anymore," I tell him so only he hears me. "I'm going to send you back to hell where no one and nothing will ever take mercy on you. Taking your life will be the greatest fucking service to the world I've ever done."

He garbles something. "What was that?"

"She was the best"–he chokes, wheezing out a laugh– "little virgin I've ever ruined." His bloodied smile is the end of my restraint.

Squeezing his throat, I watch the life drain from his eyes as my hand gets tighter and tighter. And just when he's about to slip away, I take my hand away and shove my gun in his mouth.

"You touched her. Now you die."

BANG!

Stepping back from his lifeless body, I look down at all three of them, their blood pooling on the mats a sign of my devotion to Angela – you touch her, you die.

She may not want to stay with me, but that won't stop

me from protecting her.

"Have this cleaned up," I say to no one in particular. "I'm going to pay Dom and Geno a visit."

"Luca." Leo grabs my arm, stopping me as I walk by him. "I know you have to do this. Just make sure you don't go down a hole you can't climb out of."

"It won't matter." Pulling my arm free, I keep walking, stopping outside of Dom's cell first. "Get up. Let's go," I demand. Dom blinks, his eyes adjusting to the influx of light from the hall.

"Where am I going now?"

"It's time for a family reunion." Gabriel appears, and I shove Dom at him. "Bring him to the same spot."

Opening Geno's door next, I find him sitting in the corner, his head between his knees. "Get up. Time to talk."

He lifts his head. "Fuck off."

Walking inside, I grab him by the shirt and haul him up, shoving him out the door. "Walk."

Marco is there to bring him to the gym while I stand in front of Joey's cell.

We took him to pay for having our father killed, but now it's about something so much more. I never loved my father. What we were doing was out of duty and respect, not love. But now... Now it is.

Looking through the small window in the door, I see Joey laying on a cot, his shoulder and foot bandaged. Someone must've found him after I left and called the doctor.

That call won't be happening again tonight.

Joey flinches at the sound of the door and his eyes fly open to meet mine. "What do you want now? I gave you the names. And by the blood covering you, I'd say you found them. Just kill me."

"You're about to get your wish." Stepping to the side, I hold the door open. Joey stares at me for a moment and then slowly sits up and stands.

"I can't exactly walk," he grits out, sucking in a sharp breath when he puts weight on the foot I shot.

"Does it look like I give a shit? Walk."

Cursing, Joey hobbles his way out and down the hall. "Hurry the fuck up."

"I'm trying, you bastard!" he shouts, and I shove him forward with the barrel of my gun.

"Try harder."

When we round the corner and Dom and Geno see their father for the first time since we took him, their eyes widen a fraction before hiding their reactions.

The three men I just killed have been dragged to the side, and Joey coughs out a laugh when he sees them. "So you did find them. That was quick."

"Who are they?" Geno asks.

I tilt my head to the side. "You don't recognize them? I guess you were too busy ignoring Angela's cries for help to get a good look at the men you let exploit your sister."

Dom swallows hard, and the brothers have the decency to look guilty.

"You let it happen. You never even made sure she was okay." They remain quiet. "What? Got nothing to say?"

"She was fine," Geno shrugs. "She knew what was needed of her for the family."

"Wrong answer."

BANG!

Geno just loves running his mouth.

"Fuck!" Dom yells, watching his brother drop. "What the fuck?!"

"What the fuck?" I growl. "What the fuck is right. She was alone, she was scared, and her family abandoned her. Worse, they were the reason for everything."

"I had nothing to do with it!"

"The fact that you think that is just more proof that you're a scumbag. You get to join your brother and them"–I nod to Albert, Chris, and James–"in death. Enjoy hell."

Pulling the trigger, the bullet strikes him in the forehead. This has been a night of target practice.

Turning to Joey, I tap the side of his head with my gun. "Now it's just you left. Your fate doesn't just lie with me, though." Stepping back, I see that Alec, Vinny, and Nico have joined us, and we all stand in a line before Joey.

"It looks like you had all the fun before I got here," Alec says, smirking. "You're lucky Leo called me this afternoon or I would be seriously pissed at you for having me miss this, Luca. Shit goes down, and I'm there."

"It's time to finish this," Leo says, and we all nod, turning back to Joey. "You used your daughter as a business deal closer. You had our father and their father"–he nods to Nico and Vinny–"killed. And you thought you could take what's ours. I hope you see now that Carfanos always win.

217

You fucked with the wrong family."

"I have one more thing to address," I add. "Angela thinks her mother was killed in a hit-and-run while she was out for a walk. But that's not what happened, is it?"

"The fuck?" I hear someone say under their breath.

"Is it?" I repeat.

"No," he says forcefully. "It's not. None of them wanted her anymore. And if my wife wasn't good for the one thing she wasn't even that good at…" he trails off. "There wasn't a need for her anymore."

Jesus fucking Christ. My father didn't love my mother, but he would never have whored her out or had her killed.

"The fact that you needed to hand your wife over to those men in order to close a deal is fucking pathetic. What really happened to her?"

"She was hit by a car. It just wasn't an accident."

"Fuck this, he needs to die already. I can't fucking listen to him anymore," Gabriel says.

"I was thinking the same thing," Leo announces, and we all raise our guns. "I've spent five years ruining you, breaking you down, and making you wonder when I'll finally come for you and end it. The time is now." Leo pulls his trigger first, and the rest of us follow suit, the bitter scent of gun powder filling my lungs as we empty our clips into him.

He's the last piece.

The Cicariellos are done. Over. I can sleep easy knowing none of them are going to come for Angela or anyone in my family again.

But with the end of them comes the end of her and I.

I have to let her go now.

CHAPTER 25
Angela

I haven't seen Luca in three days. I don't even think he's been back home in that time, which has my mind going to a place where he was with another woman because I pushed him away. That thought makes my heart twist.

If he was with someone else, I don't even have a right to be jealous. We're not together, and we never really were.

That doesn't make it hurt any less, though.

He said I was his, but to a man like Luca, I don't really know what that means. My mother was my father's, but he treated her like dirt.

Getting dressed, I shuffle my way out to make coffee, but startle when I see a man in the kitchen. The same man who was here to help Mrs. G.

"Hi, Angela." He smiles, raising his coffee mug.

"Who are you?" I ask tentatively, nervous.

"Nico. I'm Luca's cousin."

"Why are you here?"

Nico slides something across the kitchen island, inviting me to come closer. "Would you like a cup of coffee?" I nod, and he pours me a mug. "Cream? Sugar?"

"A little of both. Thank you."

"No problem, honey. Here you go." I take a sip and sigh, closing my eyes at how good it is. "Good?"

"Yes." I eye the envelope on the counter with my name scrawled across the front and take another sip.

"Are you going to open it?"

"I don't know if I want to know what it says."

"I think you do."

I look up at him, his eyes surprisingly warm and encouraging.

My hand trembles slightly as I reach for it, and it feels heavy in my hand as I take it to the couch, away from the eyes of Nico.

Slipping my finger beneath the sealed edge, I take out a single folded piece of paper, my heart immediately twisting.

This is it.

I unfold it, and tears immediately well in my eyes at just the sight of his beautiful handwriting.

I close my eyes, taking a breath.

I'm giving you what you want, mia uccellino.

You don't have to be afraid anymore. I took care of everything. Those men, your brothers, your father. None of them can hurt you anymore.

Fly free, my little bird.

The piece of paper shakes in my hand.

I re-read his words over and over again, trying to find more than what I'm seeing.

"I don't understand," I whisper.

"What don't you understand?" Nico asks, stepping in front of me and taking a seat on the coffee table.

"What does this mean?" I hand him the note and his eyes scan Luca's words.

"It means exactly what it says," he says carefully, looking me directly in the eyes. "They're taken care of. They can't hurt you, or anyone else, again. Ever."

"Luca killed them?" Nico remains quiet, giving me his silent yes. "How did he find them?"

"He persuaded your father to talk."

"He did?" I ask, more to myself than him, but he answers anyway.

"Luca would do anything for you," he tells me sincerely. "Which is why he's giving you what you want. You're safe now to go anywhere and do anything." He hands me another envelope, this one larger. "This has your ID, passport, and all the information you'll need to access your bank account.

There's also a new cell phone. I wrote my number on a piece of paper and slipped it inside the phone's box in case you ever need anything."

"Bank account? IDs? I don't have those."

"You do now. All of your father's and brothers' money has been transferred into an account for you. There's more than enough for you to travel, get your own place, and do whatever you want, really."

I can't believe what he's telling me.

Luca killed them. For me.

He's setting me free and gave me the means to survive on my own.

"Why didn't he tell me himself?"

"He thought it was better to stay away. But if you want my opinion"—he stands up, fixing his suit jacket—"he didn't want to watch you walk away. Now, go get whatever you want to pack and I'll drive you to the hotel where you have an open-ended reservation. You can stay as long as you'd like and check out anytime you want, if ever."

Luca did all of this for me?

He thought of everything.

Dazed, I go back to my room and pack a small bag for myself with only the essentials. I don't want to take what's not truly mine, but I need a few things to get by until I figure out what I'm doing next.

I've never been able to think of my future as my own – one where I get to choose what happens next. It's all I've ever wanted, and Luca's giving me that. And although it seems overwhelming now, I have to do this. I have to see what I can do on my own.

Shouldering the packed overnight bag, I meet Nico out in the living room.

"I'm ready," I announce, and he nods, holding the front door open for me.

When the door closes, a sharp pain flashes in my chest, making me feel like this is a goodbye I shouldn't be making. It feels like I'm leaving behind a piece of myself, but I can't go back on it now.

CHAPTER 26
Angela

Stepping out onto the sidewalk, I breathe in the cold morning air, loving the slight bite of pain from it in my lungs. It's been almost a month, and yet I still find myself looking over my shoulder, across the street, and to the left and right. For him.

And while I'm the one who wanted to leave, I still find myself wishing him to be there when I look.

I was given the world at my fingertips, and I still never left the city.

I found myself wanting to explore a place I lived for fourteen years and yet had never seen or experienced. And what I've found, is that New York City is a lonely place despite the millions of people residing here. But there's a certain comfort in the loneliness when you're alone in a sea of people.

Except I'm never alone. He's always there, just on the periphery of my mind, wanting and waiting to barge in front and center. I only let it happen at night, when I'm alone in bed, unable to sleep. Every look, touch, and word we shared floods through the walls I built when I walked out of his place that day with Nico.

Shaking my head, I flag down a taxi for a ride to this little café I discovered last month that has the best coffee and pastries.

Luca's building, and the blocks surrounding it, have been off-limits at all costs for me. I don't know what I would do if I saw him again. But after we've been driving for a few minutes, I realize where we're headed, and a slight panic sets in.

"Why are you taking this way?" I ask the driver politely.

"It's quicker, Miss."

At the next light, I bend to look out the windshield and see his building – a shiny black wall of windows reflecting the world back at whoever looks, never getting a glimpse inside.

Just like Luca.

He never let me in.

I let him see the darkest part of me, but he couldn't give me anything in return besides blood and death.

My pulse quickens the closer we get, and I spot one of his black Range Rovers out front by the curb.

Sliding closer to the window, I keep my eyes trained on

the car and building, which is when it happens. Luca walks out the front doors, his long strides to the waiting SUV full of determination and purpose. He looks the same, but different. He has a short beard covering his strong, firm jaw, that I can tell is clenched tight by the hard set of his lips.

God, I miss those lips.

And that beard… I want to know what it feels like under my hands and on my skin.

My heart squeezes in my chest, my breathing shallowing out. As my taxi passes him, his eyes lift, and I swear in that split second, he looks right at me. The glass is tinted, but I still felt them, and I start to hyperventilate, my stomach twisting in knots.

"Please," I manage to get out. "Take me back. Please," I beg the driver.

He looks at me through the rearview mirror, and I don't know what he sees, but he does as I say.

I make it back to my apartment just in time to run straight to the bathroom, throwing up last night's dinner until I'm dry heaving.

What have I done?

I've gone around pretending I'm fine for the past three weeks, when in reality, I'm miserable.

Being free isn't anything like I thought it would be.

I go around keeping myself busy by taking the subway to random neighborhoods and walking around, wandering around museums, and discovering new cafés. But it doesn't change the fact that I'm not actually happy. All I've done is create another cage for myself that I can't leave. Or rather, don't want to leave.

I checked out of the hotel after a week and into another one, not wanting Luca to know where I was or pay for anything. But I'm trapped here in the city, just hoping to find what I've been missing. I already found it, though, and I walked out on it.

I want my old, pretty cage back. I was so ready to turn my back on him and everything he gave me because all it's given me is pain and betrayal. But I don't fit in anywhere else, and I don't really want to.

I'm just living, breathing, and going about my days trying to put something, and someone, behind me who I don't even want to get over.

Rinsing my mouth out, I look at myself in the mirror. *Really* look at myself. And what I see is a shell of myself like I did for all those years.

A knock at my room door makes me practically jump out of my skin, and I approach it with caution. I don't know who it could be.

Peering through the peep hole, I breathe a sigh of relief when I see the doorman.

"Hi, Miss Cicariello," he greets when I crack the door open. "I have a delivery for you."

"I didn't order anything."

"I know, Miss. This was just delivered and I was told to bring it up to you straight away."

"What is it?" I eye the box and brown paper bag in his hands, confused.

"I don't know." He holds them out for me and I take

the items with caution.

"Thank you."

With a curt nod, he quickly turns on his heel and walks back to the bank of elevators down the hall.

Closing and locking the door, I go into the kitchen and put the box and bag down on the counter, staring at them like I'll magically see what's inside of them.

A tingling sensation crawls up my back and I know who they're from. I just don't know why, or what, it could be.

I haven't heard anything from him since I left.

I don't know what I expected, but I guess it wasn't to be cut off.

A part of me held onto the hope that he would fight for me. I know that's more than I had a right to want, though. Luca took me away from a life that gave me nothing but nightmares and gave me one that, no matter how brief, was a safe harbor to let me be myself. He didn't ask me to be anyone but me. I was the one who wanted to run.

I start with the bag. Unfolding the opening, I look inside and tears gather in my eyes. I pull out a container of tomato soup, a loaf of fresh bread that looks to be from the bakery like in his apartment, and a package of sliced cheddar cheese.

Why would he send me this?

Opening the box next, there's an envelope resting on top of the tissue paper with my name written across it just like he left for me that morning.

On a deep breath, I slip my finger under the edge and pull out the folded piece of paper.

There's a storm coming tonight and I want you to have this so you know I'm there with you. You're strong enough on your own, but I still want to be there with you.

The words blur in front of me as tears roll down my cheeks. Peeling apart the tissue paper, I choke on a sob, covering my face with my hands.

He didn't.

Swiping the tears away, I smooth the tips of my fingers over the fabric.

He gave me his jacket back.

I left it folded under my pillow when I left, which means he went in there. He looked. I still never told him why I kept it, but I guess I didn't need to. He already knew. He seems to know what I need without me ever having to say anything.

Pulling it to my nose, I inhale the collar of his suit jacket and cry even harder.

It smells just like him. Stronger even. He must've worn it again before sending it to me.

He thought of me.

He thought of everything.

My knees aren't able to hold me up any longer and I slide down the side of the kitchen island, burying my face in his jacket.

The truth, I'm starting to realize, is that all I wanted was a choice. I just wanted a choice in how I got to live my life. I didn't want to be forced anymore.

I made the choice I needed to at the time, but I want to

fly home. I want to fly back to the man who gave me the chance to have a choice.

I wanted to believe him when he said I was his, but I couldn't fathom someone accepting me after admitting what happened.

He did, though. He still wanted me. And he killed everyone who ever hurt me so I'd feel safe when he let me go.

I've never known a mafia man to love anyone other than himself, but what he did for me…I think it was his way of telling me how he felt.

And I still walked away.

* * * *

I ate the soup and made myself a grilled cheese just as the rain was starting, but now the late fall thunderstorm rumbles loudly outside. Curling into Luca's jacket, the fabric and scent weave their magic around me, and I can feel him here with me.

I'm not afraid to close my eyes, knowing I have a piece of him with me. Sleep comes easy for the first time since I left, and I don't wake once, nor do I have a single nightmare.

Luca gave me back my safety. He gave me back him.

* * * *

I thought this would be a good idea, but now I'm seriously second guessing myself.

I gave the taxi driver the address and now we've been parked outside of Luca's building for ten minutes, trying to get my stomach to unknot, my palms to stop sweating, and my head to stop spinning.

"Miss?"

"Yes, sorry. Just one more minute." I told him to let the meter run, not caring about the money in the least.

I hear him sigh, but I don't care about him either.

I'm never going to be any less nervous than I am now, so I hand him a few bills and climb out of the cab, my future in front of me.

It feels like I'm being watched from every angle, but I keep my head up, tamping down my paranoia.

The doorman gives me a small nod in greeting that I return with a mumbled hello as I pass. The cold lobby is black and white with gold accents, and the heels of my boots click on the marble floor as I walk towards a man behind the front desk, making me feel even more like I'm being watched.

"Can I help you?" he asks, his face devoid of emotions. He's clearly meant to keep everyone away.

"Yes, is Luca here?"

The man eyes me with a narrowed stare, and I place my hands on the raised ledge of his desk.

"And you are?" he practically sneers.

"Angela Cicariello."

His face immediately pales, and the corners of my mouth tilt up, loving that my name put that scared look on his face. I feel empowered.

"Let me make a call."

I hear him pressing the buttons on his desk phone, but the ding of the elevator arriving sends a chill through me and my eyes stay fixed on the doors that are sliding open.

Luca steps off, his eyes already locked on mine from across the way. I feel them like a bolt of lightning hitting my heart and bursting through me with a new energy.

I'm rooted where I stand, unable to move.

CHAPTER 27
Luca

I don't know how much longer I can stay away.

It's been almost a month and she never left the fucking city. I gave her everything she needed to go as far away as she wanted, and she never left.

I want to believe it's because of me, but that's just me being a selfish bastard.

Gio, the guy I've had tailing her, tells me every time she leaves her hotel and where she goes. I expect the worst every time – to hear she's out with some other guy. If I ever got that report, she'd be in for a rude fucking awakening. I let her go, but no man will touch her but me. No one else gets to know her secrets. No one else gets to hold her. No one else gets to fuck her.

I already know I'm selfish, and I already know I have no right to claim her. But I'm aware of it, which means my crazy is actually the sanest part of me.

When I checked the weather a few days ago and saw a huge rainstorm was headed for the city, I couldn't fathom her bearing it alone.

I know she can, and has, but the thought of her huddled on the bathroom floor trying to drown out the memories is something I refuse to let happen.

The first night she was gone, I returned to my place, only to find the silence and emptiness a new form of torture I was going to have to endure.

Gio reported in yesterday that she left her hotel in a taxi and drove past my building. I was exiting and getting into my car, and after passing me, her taxi turned on the next block and looped right back around to her hotel. He saw her run inside and she didn't come back out.

I was fucking ecstatic.

I still had her.

That first night alone, I sat on her bed and inhaled her scent she had imbedded in everything she touched. That's when I found my jacket still folded neatly under her pillow, and when I saw there'd be a storm in a few days, an idea struck me. I wore it yesterday, then boxed it up and sent it, along with a meal I know will bring her comfort, to her hotel room.

If she was surprised I knew where she lived after checking out of the room I had reserved for her, she shouldn't have been.

All last night, I sat outside her building, wanting to be nearby in case she needed me. I knew she wouldn't have a way to even know I was out there, but I still needed to be close.

"Luca, are you listening?"

"No," I say without thought, and Leo slams his hand down on the table.

"We're discussing Katarina."

"What about her?"

"It's time to find her someone."

"Do you have any ideas on who? She's our baby sister. We're not handing her over to a man who will treat her like shit and a piece of property."

Leo eyes me. "You know I would never fucking allow that. Katarina deserves a goddamn prince or king, but I already looked it up, and there's none available."

"Is there a deal we want with anyone?" It's customary to marry off the women in the family to broker a deal with another. Our mother is a Melcciona. She was given to our father so they'd have an in with the most powerful family, and we got their premium dock properties.

If our father was alive, he'd marry her to whoever he wanted. But Katarina is special to us. We've watched out for her our entire lives. She's not just going to be handed off to some asshole.

"The Antonuccis reached out. Santino is 28 and in line to take over. After Joey, Dom, and Geno, they want to stay on good ground with us, so they're offering to merge their food trucking company with ours. We'd have control over the food and garment industries, then."

"Is he good enough for Kat?"

"He hasn't come up on my radar yet, which is good. I want to set a meeting next month so we can meet him and discuss things."

"Have you told Kat anything yet?"

"No. She doesn't know, and she won't until I decide on him."

"She's not going to like it either way."

"I know. But I'm not letting her go out and date some mook who won't be able to give her what she deserves. If we have a merger with them, she'll always be a part of us. She'll always be a Carfano, regardless of what last name she takes."

"Of course she will." Leaning back in my chair, I take a sip from my coffee cup. "The two of us should be enough to ensure they know we're not fucking around with our sister. It's not like how Dom and Geno viewed Angela." My chest tightens at saying her name.

"We're not them, Luca."

"No, we're not." But she thinks we are.

My phone vibrates in my pocket, and when I pull it out, I see Stefano's name on my screen.

"What do you need?" I answer.

"Don't bite my head off," he replies. "She's here."

I freeze.

"Who's here?" I ask carefully, getting Leo's attention.

"Angela just got out of a cab and is walking towards the front doors."

Hanging up, I push out of my chair with enough force to send it flying, and run to the elevators.

I had Stef set up facial recognition on our security cameras to flag Angela if she comes anywhere near our building. And here she is, walking right inside.

I can't even fucking think straight right now. All I can do is get to her as fast as I can.

I need to see her.

It feels like the elevator ride is the longest of my life as I watch the numbers descend. When the doors finally open, my heart beats like a fucking drum so all I can hear is the beat, all I can see is her, and all I can think is *mine*.

She's beautiful. Beyond anything this world should even know. And she came back.

Her eyes lock with mine – two stars ready to guide me home. To her.

She doesn't make a move towards me. In fact, I don't even know if she's breathing. But I can see it all right there in her look.

Everything I want. It's all right there in her eyes.

Striding towards her, my world narrows with each step until she's the only thing in it.

I stop in front of her, my hands itching to reach out and touch her, but I resist. "*Mia uccellino.*" On my whispered sentiment, Angela's eyes melt into pools of honey and her lips part on a sigh. "You're here."

"Yes, I…" she trails off, swallowing hard. "I…" Her nerves are getting the better of her and I see doubt flash in her eyes, so I reach out and run the backs of my fingers

237

across her cheek, sliding my hand into her hair.

Closing her eyes, Angela takes a deep breath and I feel her relax. When her eyes open again, I see everything she's feeling.

"Thank you for the gifts last night." Her soft voice floats into me. "I didn't wake up once or have a nightmare."

"I would've rather been there myself."

"Me too," she admits, her eyes darting down to my lips and then back up.

"Why are you here? Tell me what you want, Angela."

"You." Before she even finishes the word, my mouth slams down, fusing my lips to hers.

Fuck me.

Plunging my tongue into her mouth, I sweep mine against hers, her sweetness tasting like fucking sunshine after a month of darkness.

Moaning, Angela grips the front of my shirt in her fists and pulls me closer.

Jesus Christ, I missed her.

Growling, I lift her up and toss her over my shoulder, stalking back to the elevator. When the doors close, I slide her down my front and pin her to the wall, kissing her gasp of surprise away.

I need to touch her.

I need more, and I can't wait.

Unbuttoning her skin tight jeans, I slide the zipper down and shove my hand inside her panties, groaning at finding her soaking wet.

Nipping her lip, I circle her clit and press down hard, her

moan my undoing as it vibrates through me. Slipping two fingers inside her tight pussy, I stretch them out and then hook them towards me, pulling her forward.

"I'm not going to be able to hold back, Angela. Once we walk through my door, that's it. There's no going back. There's no walking away again. You'll be mine. Fully. In every way. Forever."

Her eyes light up and I stroke her front wall while rubbing light circles around her clit. She blinks rapidly, a glazed look coming over her.

"Do you understand?"

She blinks again, her eyes clearer. "Yes," she sighs. "I want to be yours, Luca."

The sweetest fucking words ever spoken.

The elevator dings open and I remove my hand from her panties, Angela's choked moan making my pulse race.

"Don't worry, *uccellino*, you'll get more soon."

"Please," she begs, and I groan, tossing her over my shoulder again.

Stalking through my house, I walk her straight back to my room and toss her down on the bed.

"We'll talk after. Right now, I need you too fucking badly."

"Please," she begs again, and I flash her a grin.

"I love when you beg, baby."

I can't shed our clothes fast enough, and when I have her naked before me, I only give myself a fraction of a second to appreciate her before I'm covering her with kisses and parting her legs, settling between her smooth thighs.

"I've dreamt of this," I tell her, plunging my cock into her wet center.

Fuck, she's tight. Her pussy is strangling me and I know I'm not going to last long.

"Me too," I hear her say softly, and my eyes snap to hers. I see the sincerity in them, and I want to make sure she knows who's going to own her, body and soul, for the rest of her life.

Pulling out slowly, I watch her face morph with pleasure, letting her feel all of me inside of her. But when she squeezes me, I can't hold back any longer. I haven't had her in weeks, and I didn't know when I would again.

I slam into her, and I'm home. Her heat welcomes me back where I belong and I lose myself in her.

Her tits jiggle with every thrust, her mouth hangs open while her moans and sighs escape, and her skin flushes a beautiful shade of pink.

She's amazing. Perfect. Beautiful. A fucking princess deserving of a crown to stand beside me. She was just a little broken bird when I found her, and here she is, risen from the ashes like a phoenix – a beautiful and rare bird all her own. Special and unique, and for my eyes only.

I know she's close. I can feel the walls of her pussy start to spasm around me.

"I'm not going to pull out this time, Angela," I growl. "I'm going to fill you up with my come and make sure you're mine in every way."

Angela's eyes light up, loving the idea as much as me, and it drives me to fuck her harder.

"Keep your eyes on me," I demand. "I need them."

She peels her eyes open, and when they meet mine, that's all it takes for her to detonate around me. Arching off the bed, she grips the sheets and screams out her release. My favorite music.

Her pussy clamps down on me like a fucking vice, pulling my own release from me. I still inside of her, making good on my promise. I coat her walls with my come, making sure she's filled and overflowing with our mixed juices.

Kissing the dusty rose tips of her nipples, I kiss my way up her chest and throat until I'm hovering just above her lips. "Thank you for coming back, *mia uccellino*."

CHAPTER 28
Angela

Being in Luca's arms again feels like home.

He's my home.

I've never had a home, and now no matter where I am, so long as I have Luca, I'll know I'm home.

Grazing my fingers up his side, I rest them on his firm chest, his heart beat in sync with mine.

"I never wanted to leave you, Luca."

"Then why did you?"

"Because I needed to know what it would be like to be on my own. It was all I wanted. Until…"

"Until what?" He traces gentle circles around my chest and down my arm with the ghost of a smile tilting the corners of his mouth up.

"Until you. You were my safe harbor in a storm that was always raging around me. You guided me out of the storm, and it was in that calm that I realized how scared I was. I still am."

"Of what, baby?"

"You. Me. Me and you. All of this. I don't know what it means to be with someone. I don't know how to love someone." I pinch my eyes closed, hoping he didn't catch my confession for what it was.

"Open your eyes, *uccellino*," he urges, lifting my chin.

I do as he says, and when I look into his again, I see exactly how I'm feeling reflected in his eyes.

"You don't have to ever worry about any of that. I want you as you are. Give me all of you, and I'll give you all of me in return. As long as we have each other, the rest of the world can fuck-off. Nothing and no one will come between us. I promise you that. *Tu sei il mio mondo ora.*"

My heart constricts.

"You are my world now, Angela." He leans his forehead against mine, his lips almost grazing mine. "I love you, *mia uccellino. Ti amo.*"

Tears pool in my eyes and spill down my cheeks, but Luca cups my face and kisses them away.

"I love you," I whisper, my voice raw from too many emotions clogging my throat.

Kissing me slowly, Luca licks my tears from my lips and then pulls back to look at me.

I see love shining within his dark chocolate pools, and I

want to look into those eyes for the rest of my life.

"Why did you let me go? You said I was yours and yet you let me go."

"Trust me when I say I wanted to make you stay. But I couldn't. You know that saying – if you love something, set it free, and if it was meant to be, it'll come back."

"I guess we're meant to be."

"I knew it the moment I kicked your door down and saw you standing there."

"You killed them," I whisper.

His jaw clenches. "I did."

Reaching up, I trace my fingers down the side of his handsome face. "Thank you."

"I know I'm probably going to fuck this up again, but just know that no matter what, I'm going to put you before anything and everyone else. You deserve the world, and I'm going to give it to you. You have a clean slate, baby. You can do anything and be anything you want."

"Right now, I just want to be yours. I am going to want to finish my Art History degree though, and try and get a job at a gallery or museum, but right now…"

"You know I'm going to want to keep you tied up at all times, waiting for me so I can have a taste of you whenever I want, right?"

"You don't have to keep me tied up for that."

Groaning, Luca captures my lips in a hard kiss and cups my breast, pinching my nipple.

"And we have connections with galleries. You can have your pick, baby."

"You'd let me work? Leave the house?"

"You sound surprised."

"I am."

"I don't want to keep you locked away, Angela. I just want you safe. As long as you have one of my men with you when you go out, then you can do anything you'd like. I just can't give you a life of pure freedom. That will never be possible."

"I think I can deal with that. I don't want to run, Luca. I just want a choice. I've always only wanted a choice. And I choose you."

"You were chosen for me, *uccellino*. You're the best decision I never had control over, and I'm a man who likes control." He smirks.

"I've noticed."

"You want another demonstration of it?"

"I do." I smile, and Luca traces my lips, an odd look on his face. "What's wrong?"

"I've been wanting to know what you'd look like smiling."

"I've never really had a reason to."

"I promise to make sure you have more reasons to."

"You never smile," I tell him, tracing his lips like he did mine.

"I've never had a reason to," he says, using my words.

"Hmm, I wonder if you'd be even more handsome smiling. I don't know, though, because your brooding stony nature is pretty sexy."

His lips twitch before he gives me a full-blown smile that

makes my heart stop momentarily. "You think I'm sexy, *uccellino?*"

"Yes," I breathe, unable to process how damn handsome he is.

"I think you're pretty sexy too, baby." He smirks, sliding his hands down my sides. "Every inch of you."

"Show me," I taunt, sliding my hand down between us to grip him. "Show me what you think of me."

Luca's eyes light up.

Pressing me back into the mattress, he crawls down my body, his broad shoulders parting my legs.

"I'll show you every day." His hot tongue licks my folds and I'm gone.

Luca Carfano and I would've never met had my father not had his killed. That single act of violence set in motion a series of events that eventually led him to me.

Violence was the beginning and middle of our story, but it's not the end.

The future is ours to carve out.

ACKNOWLEDGMENTS

THANK YOU to each and every one of my readers! The fact that you pick up my books and (hopefully) love getting lost in my characters and stories, amazes me! Every time I hear one of you say that you stayed up all night reading my books and can't wait for the next one, it fills me with such happiness and reminds me why I started on this journey. I hope you enjoyed Luca and Angela, and I'll see you back in the acknowledgments section in my next book!

ABOUT THE AUTHOR

Rebecca is a dreamer through and through with permanent wanderlust. She has an endless list of places to go and see, hoping to one day experience the world and all it has to offer.

She's a Jersey girl who dreams of living in a place with freezing cold winters and lots of snow! When she's not writing, you can find her planning her next road trip and drinking copious amounts of coffee (preferably iced!).

newsletter, blog, shop, and links to all social media:
www.rebeccagannon.com

Follow me on Instagram to stay up-to-date on new releases, sales, teasers, giveaways, and so much more!
@rebeccagannon_author

Printed in Great Britain
by Amazon

44404238R00148